MY SISTER THE VAMPIRE

Vampire School Dropout?

More

MY SISTER THE VAMPIRE

MY SISTER THE VAMPIRE

Vampire School Dropout?

Sienna Mercer

SCHOLASTIC INC.

With special thanks to Chandler Craig

ISBN 978-0-545-39143-6

Copyright © 2012 by Working Partners Ltd.
Series created by Working Partners Ltd., London. All rights reserved.
Published by Scholastic Inc., 557 Broadway, New York, NY 10012,
by arrangement with Working Partners Ltd.
SCHOLASTIC and associated logos are
trademarks and/or registered trademarks of Scholastic Inc.

12 11 10 9 8 7 6 5 4 3 2 1   12 13 14 15 16 17/0

Printed in the U.S.A.   40

First Scholastic printing, September 2012

Typography by Joel Tippie

For Rob, for being my best friend

Ivy leaned back in her swivel chair and lifted her shiny black combat boots up onto the oak desk. Her grandparents had given her the desk on her first day at the new überfancy boarding school she was attending.

CHAPTER 1

Ivy leaned back in her swivel chair and lifted her shiny black combat boots up onto the oak desk. Her grandparents had given her the desk on her first day at the new überfancy boarding school she was attending.

"You cannot get a proper education at a proper school without a proper place to work," Count and Countess Lazar had told her. Apparently an antique desk weighing as much as a small freight train was the only thing that would do. There were miniature bats carved into the rich mahogany and iron drawer handles in V shapes. Ivy leaned over and tapped the bottom of the desk. A secret

1

compartment opened up, out of which she pulled her shiny new student ID, complete with the awkward picture of her curling her lips into an odd mix between a smile and a scowl.

She'd agonized over the decision to enroll at Wallachia Academy in Transylvania. It wasn't easy being a vampire, but a teen vampire whose powers were on a sudden growth spurt? That was even more challenging. Her grandparents had suggested boarding at the same academy where generations of her family had learned to hone their super-strong powers. Ivy had only two problems with this—she didn't want to leave her twin sister, Olivia, and no way did she want to be apart from Brendan, her boyfriend. But in the end, she'd been persuaded to leave Franklin Grove. "And I'm going to make the most of this," she muttered to herself, gazing out over the lawns. "Whatever it takes."

She flipped open her laptop, tapping the space bar so that the screen lit up. Her grandparents had done a killer job making sure she'd settled in when she'd first arrived at Wallachia Academy. Of course, they'd brought the family butler, Horatio, to do all the heavy lifting. *Thank darkness they did! Olivia insisted on packing my entire wardrobe!* Olivia could have saved herself the time, since Ivy was stuck wearing the school uniform every day. It was pretty formal—a crimson pleated skirt and a black sweater emblazoned with the Wallachia Academy crest—although she had managed to "Ivy up" the outfit with her signature boots and a chopstick-pinned bun. *Hoity-toity school or not, Ivy is staying Ivy,* she thought.

She glanced at her schedule for the first day of school, which hung above her desk.

9 o'clock Etiquette
10 o'clock Potion Mixing
11 o'clock Fang Maintenance
1 o'clock Herbal Science
2 o'clock Coffin Carpentry

And she had thought woodshop class at Franklin Grove was bad!

Ivy typed her password and signed on to the Vorld Vide Veb, the secret vampy version of the Internet. She clicked her mouse and opened up the Lonely Echo webcam program. She'd been using their vampire video chat software to talk to Olivia, but seeing her sister's face flash up on the monitor each time had done nothing to help her homesickness. *I just can't stop calling her, even though it makes me feel worse afterward.* Sometimes being one-half of a set of twins was really difficult. She clicked on Olivia's avatar and waited for the connection to kick in. She hadn't spoken to her grandparents at all since arriving at the Academy a few days ago. She'd chatted with her father, Charles, only once. *No wonder I keep calling Olivia. I need* some *contact with the outside world!*

Static blinked across the screen. *Something's happening!* Ivy sat up straighter. A sharp picture appeared on the monitor. A bright Franklin Grove day shone through the open set of French doors that led out into Olivia's backyard. Ivy could practically smell the freshly mowed lawns and newly potted pansies from clear across the Atlantic.

"One second!" she heard a voice call from offscreen.

Ivy tapped her black nails on the surface of her desk. Olivia was a full six hours behind her, so while it was first thing in the morning for Ivy's twin, outside Ivy's window in Transylvania the sun was already setting. Trees cast long shadows across the school grounds; the light outside had grown dim and fuzzy. Turrets spiraled up into the evening sky, and on the ground below teachers in long black gowns scurried to their quarters. Ivy switched on her desk lamp.

Who would have thought Ivy Vega would be nostalgic at the sight of a little sun? *I'm a vampire, for darkness' sake!* Pitch-black was kind of supposed to be her *thing*. But she couldn't help that she missed her hometown. She hadn't been 100 percent sure she'd wanted to attend Wallachia in the first place, even if it was tradition in elite vampire society.

Olivia's adoptive dad, Mr. Abbott, suddenly entered the frame on Ivy's laptop. He was wrapped in a white bathrobe with the sash tied around his forehead. He was several feet away from the camera lens, in the middle of Olivia's backyard, struggling to position two stools side by side and lay a plank of wood across the top. *This does not look good.* Ivy knew that Olivia's dad was an amateur karate *gi*—was he going through his routines now? Ivy tried to stay very still so that he wouldn't notice her image on the computer screen. *I don't want to disturb him. If he breaks any bones, it won't be my fault.*

He took three steps back, slipping momentarily out of the picture, before charging forward, arms raised in the air like a deranged whooping crane. *"Hiiiiiyyaaaaaaaah!"* he screamed, slamming the side of his hand down on the wood plank.

Ivy cringed as Mr. Abbott came away shaking his red karate-chopping hand. He picked up the plank and turned it around. *As if that's going to help,* Ivy thought. She wanted to cover her eyes but it was like a car wreck she couldn't stop watching. He wound up again, preparing for his running start. *"Hiiiiiiyyaaaaaaah!"* he repeated. This time his hand smacked the plank with such force that he lost his footing and slipped backward, falling hard on the garden mulch.

"Sorry about that!" Olivia popped into the frame. She was stirring a bowl of cereal with a spoon. Her hair was pulled back into a sleek ponytail and she had a bright purple scarf around her neck. "Now, where were we?"

"Um, Olivia?" Ivy pointed over her twin's shoulder. "Is your dad okay?"

Mr. Abbott was struggling to roll over. The white sash tied around his forehead had fallen down over his eyes. "Did I break it?" he moaned, crawling to his feet.

"Not this time," called Olivia happily from just within the open French doors, before turning to whisper to Ivy. "Don't worry. He's trying to earn his yellow belt. He's been working on that plank all week and hasn't broken a finger yet." She shrugged. "So, how's it going?"

"Well," Ivy said, scooping up her laptop, "shall I give you the grand tour?"

"Absolutely! Except right now the only thing I can see is a close-up of your cheek."

"Oops, sorry." Ivy pulled the laptop lens away from her face. She'd been cradling it as she spun in her chair. She angled the screen to face the room. "Better?"

"Much!"

"Here's my closet." Ivy tried to do a quick sweep of the camera across the mess that was her closet, but her sister wasn't going to be fooled.

"Ivy Vega!" Olivia exclaimed. "Is that *your* closet? It looks like a natural disaster hit it! Go back, go back—I want to see the full horror." Reluctantly, Ivy turned the camera back on her closet. Crumpled T-shirts, skinny jeans, and leggings littered the floor.

"It's not my fault!" Ivy protested. "It's cramped in here. See?" She did a grand gesture with her arm. "This is the rest of my room. Well, *my* room that I share with five other girls." She showed Olivia the row of coffins that were arranged one on top of another on wooden stilts, like extra-special bunk beds.

Photo collages of her roommates and cool vintage posters of black-and-white Hollywood movies were plastered above the coffins, and each girl had a silver name plaque engraved in fancy script—*Petra, Katrina, Anastasia, Alexandra, Galina,* and *Ivy.* Ivy had personalized her space by taping up a strip of Polaroid pictures that she, Brendan, and Olivia had taken in the photo booth outside the Franklin Grove movie theater. Ivy was in the middle, making an exaggerated face of disgust, while Brendan and Olivia were kissing her cheeks on either side, smooshing her face in. *Good times,* thought Ivy, with a sudden twist in the pit of her stomach.

"Oooooh," Olivia gushed. "You have room-mates! How do you like them? Do you stay up late and gossip or play Secrets and Lies?" Olivia was remembering the vampire game they had played together at Tessa's bachelorette party.

Ivy frowned. "They're okay. But it's not exactly an Ivy-friendly setup, if you know what I mean. Six girls, six coffins. That means lots of chatter, especially after nails in."

"'Nails in'?" echoed Olivia.

"The vamp version of 'lights out,'" explained Ivy, turning the camera back on herself.

"Ah." Olivia giggled. "You're not exactly Miss Sunshine most days, but a *sleep-deprived* Ivy? I bet that could scare even the most hardened vampire!" At that, Olivia's eyes went as wide as a character in an anime—not that Ivy could find any anime in Transylvania. It was all classic Russian novels and Victorian poetry.

"Okay, okay. Ha-ha. Enough with the fake

shocked look." Ivy rolled her darkly lined eyes. "Surely I'm not *that* scary, especially not from several thousand miles away and through a laptop."

Olivia's eyes were still round, and now she was shaking her head slowly. "No, it's not that," she said in a hushed voice. "I don't want to scare you, but . . ." She touched her finger to the screen. "I think there's a bat in your dorm room!"

Ivy swiveled to check out the bat perched on top of the armoire. Its paper-thin wings were wrapped around its fuzzy brown body and its pointy ears stuck out from its head like an elf's. She shrugged. "Oh, don't worry. That's just Ivan."

"Ivan?" Olivia wrinkled her nose as if she'd just smelled day-old garbage.

"Yeah, everyone gets a bat on their first day at Wallachia. He's harmless, but a little—what's the word I'm looking for?" She pressed a finger into her dimple, like she was thinking hard. *"Bitey."*

Olivia shuddered. At least, Ivy thought it was a shudder, but it could have been a glitch in the Internet connection. Ivy was already getting tired of dealing with the difficulties of overseas communication. "No offense," Olivia was saying, "but if that's the case, I might not be in a hurry to visit!"

Ivy swallowed hard. She knew her sister was joking, but she didn't want Olivia to see that her joke had made her feel instantly homesick. "Anyway," Ivy said, trying to sound natural. "The bell for dinner is going to go off soon. Will you be online later?"

"Probably. I promised I'd help our bio-dad with some sort of 'research project.'" Olivia curved her fingers into air quotes. "Whatever that means. It'll only take a few hours and then I'll be back later," she continued, waving. "Oh, and, Ivy?"

Ivy leaned forward in her chair. "Yeah?"

"I miss you."

Ivy gave a weak smile and nodded in return. "I miss you, too." Her stomach crawled up her throat as she reached for the mouse on her laptop.

"Ciao!"

The chat window went black, and Ivy shut down her computer. It wasn't that she didn't like Wallachia; it was just that she *really* liked Franklin

Grove. Ivy grabbed her cable-knit sweater with the Wallachia crest off the back of the chair. She patted Ivan on the head, snatching her hand back when he tried to nip at her. "Watch it!" she said, glaring at the beady-eyed bat. *My fingers will* not *make a tasty snack!* she thought, sending silent messages to the small, leathery mammal. *Don't even try me.*

"I'm out of here," she said, heading for the door. There was no point in staying all alone, pining for Franklin Grove. Not with a whole school to explore!

★ 🦇 ★

The Wallachia Academy dining room was fancier than most of the restaurants Ivy had been to in her entire life. Round granite tables sprinkled the banquet hall, dappled with the light of a dozen sparkling chandeliers. Crystal goblets cast multicolored prisms onto the luxurious cream tablecloths. The tables had been set with antique silverware and china nicer than the best stuff her father kept in their cabinets at home!

Petra, a fellow classmate whom Ivy had met as a guest at the vampire royal wedding, waved her over to a nearby table. Three slices of barely touched flank steak were piled on Petra's plate, dripping in a creamy white sauce that made Ivy's mouth water.

"Hey, Ivy." A cool vintage pendant dangled from Petra's neck. "Did you get in trouble today?" Petra Tarasov wasn't like some of the other snobzillas at Wallachia, but Ivy still found her a bit hard to get to know. She was friendly enough, but it was almost as though there was an invisible wall between them, some secret that Ivy didn't know. Petra had glossy brown hair that swooped down to the middle of her back, and there was always some piece of her Wallachia wardrobe that was a touch funky or offbeat. Petra didn't seem ready to morph into a Wallachia clone—that gave them something in common, at least.

"Trouble? Why would I have gotten in trouble?" Ivy asked, sliding to the edge of her seat.

Petra raised her eyebrows. "Oh, I don't know." She shrugged. "Just something I heard— that's all."

Ivy narrowed her eyes. "Something you heard? Okay . . ." Being cautious was clearly still the way to go with Petra. Ivy tried not to be irritated. Everyone had their own odd ways. Olivia was always reminding her to look for the best in people. Ivy could hear her now: "Everyone has a ray of sunshine in their heart, Ivy. You just need to find it." Normally a speech like that would have had Ivy gagging—but not anymore. *I swear I'll never make another sarcastic comment ever again if I get back to Franklin Grove.*

A group of vamp girls was gathered around an open laptop propped up on one of the tables, giggling in high-pitched voices. Ivy caught a glimpse of a bright white smile and some tousled blond hair on-screen. Petra clucked her tongue and rolled her eyes. "Ridiculous," she said. "Isn't it?"

"What's ridiculous?" Ivy craned her neck, but she couldn't make out whatever was on the screen. Vampires, and especially Wallachia Academy vampires, were supposed to be the most super-cool beings in the world. Acting aloof was practically a national sport. So, what could possibly be so amusing that it had reduced Ivy's classmates into a group of giggling girly-girls?

Petra flicked her wrist, as if she were brushing

away the whole scene. "It probably has to do with that American actor who announced he was single today. Now they can all go and daydream about having a shot with him." She pressed her palms together and held them to the side of her head like she was dreaming.

American actor . . . ? Ivy grabbed Petra's arm so forcefully she nearly pulled her right out of her chair. "Which actor?" She shook her.

Petra looked surprised. "Wow, you really need to get those powers under control. That blond-haired pretty boy—what's-his-face." She snapped her fingers, thinking. "Jackson something?"

"No!" Ivy let go of her arm, and Petra swiftly pulled it away. "Not Jackson! Jackson Caulfield?" Olivia hadn't said a word on the videophone. She hadn't even looked unhappy!

"Obsessed much?" A white-coated member of the Wallachia kitchen staff came over with a pitcher of O-negative and filled their crystal goblets with the bright red liquid. "I don't know why the sudden interest," the woman went on. "It wasn't even a good breakup. The press release called it 'amicable.' Where's the fun in that?"

"The fun?!" Ivy squeaked. "There is no fun!" Petra stared at Ivy like she had squid tentacles coming out of her ears, but Ivy didn't have time to explain. She bolted from the dining room, sprinting vampire-fast back to her dorm, up the stone stairs, and along a corridor with oil paintings hanging on the wood-paneled walls.

She slammed the door shut, jumped into her swivel chair, and fired up Lonely Echo on her computer. "Olivia?" She jostled the mouse. "Olivia?" But all Ivy could see was a blank image of Olivia's yard. No Olivia in sight. Ivy's heart did a nosedive.

Her poor sister had been brokenhearted and Ivy had spent the entire conversation talking about herself, showing Olivia stupid piles of clothes. *What kind of a twin am I?* She was supposed to have a sixth sense about this sort of thing. But more important, why hadn't Olivia mentioned anything? It wasn't like her to keep her emotions bottled up—that was more Ivy's specialty.

The sound of footsteps came through the monitor from Olivia's backyard. Ivy leaned in to listen, breathing a sigh of relief. Her sister was coming back, after all. "Hey, Olivia!" she called. "Why didn't you tell me about you and Ja—"

"Oh, hello, Ivy." Mr. Abbott's face appeared upside down on the screen as he leaned over the computer from above, and Ivy nearly bit her tongue trying to stop herself from saying the J-word.

"Um . . . um . . . Hi, Mr. Abbott," Ivy stammered. He held up one finger to tell her to wait. He wandered around to the front of the computer so that his image was now the right way around.

"Ah, that's better," Mr. Abbott said, adjusting the screen.

Ivy was glad to see that he had changed out of his karate gear and was now dressed in a maroon sweater vest and pleated khaki pants—much more appropriate suburban dad wear. "Good to see you, Ivy. How's that fancy boarding school of yours? Are you enjoying it?"

"Yeah, yeah. Definitely," said Ivy quickly, trying to peek around Mr. Abbott's head, which seemed to take up the entire frame. "Where's Olivia?" she asked before he could introduce any more questions of his own.

"Olivia?" Mr. Abbott rubbed his chin, glancing back toward the house. "She went to take a nap. She's been quite sleepy lately. She's had a busy few days, I think."

Ivy felt more rotten than week-old milk. She knew exactly why Olivia was suddenly feeling so run-down, but Mr. Abbott obviously didn't. Unfortunately, she couldn't fill him in. It would be going against twin code and it wasn't her place to tell Olivia's dad about the breakup.

"Okay, Mr. Abbott." Ivy sighed. "I guess I'll catch up with her later, then."

Ivy was stretching out to close down the chat window when he asked, "So, what's new with school?"

Ivy froze, trying not to wince. Mr. Abbott could be really chatty. Reluctantly, she plopped back into her chair, but Olivia's dad was no longer looking at her expectantly. "Shhh!" he told her, pressing his finger up to his pursed lips. His eyes were fixed on something behind Ivy. "I don't want to scare you," he said in a whisper. "But I think I see a bat in your room."

Ivy started to tell him not to worry, but stopped

short. "You know"—she leaned closer to switch the computer off while she had a chance—"I better take care of that! Um . . . hey, can anyone help?" She stood up, sending her chair clattering back, waving her hands to beckon imaginary friends in from the hallway. "Come quick— there's a bat in my room!" Mr. Abbott didn't have to know that the scrawny little creature didn't scare Ivy at all—at least not since she'd gotten fast enough to avoid having her fingers bitten. "I'm really going to have to sign off now!" Ivy panted as she widened her eyes in mock terror.

"Ivy, are you all right . . . ?" Mr. Abbott started to ask.

"I'll be fine. I should just really go now!" With a neat snap, she switched off the monitor and sank back into her chair. "Good-bye, Mr. Abbott," she murmured, shaking her head. *The things I do to keep Olivia's secrets!*

CHAPTER 2

TEEN GIRLS EVERYWHERE CELEBRATE! JACKSON CAULFIELD IS SINGLE AT LAST!

Olivia plopped the open magazine down on her bed. *Aren't breakups hard enough* without *the public humiliation?* At least for once the tabloids weren't lying. Her breakup with Jackson *had* been amicable, but Olivia couldn't help feeling pangs of sadness every time she stopped to think about it for too long. One thing was for sure: This whole ordeal was making her seriously rethink her subscription to *Star-Studded Magazine*.

Olivia's phone vibrated on her nightstand. She picked it up and saw there was a text from

Jackson. It read: "You okay?"

Olivia leaned her head back on her comfy down pillows. "Not really," she started to type, but then deleted it with one push of her thumb. She was not going to play Little Miss Damsel in Distress. Olivia might have been an up-and-coming thespian, but that was the last role she wanted. It wasn't easy to admit, but looking back, she could see that her relationship with her boyfriend—ex-boyfriend—had been going downhill for a while. *Even if I hadn't wanted to admit it to myself—or to him.* Jackson had been busy on his promotional tours and there had been little time left for them to spend together. The phone calls became fewer and further apart. The e-mails got shorter.

Then, on her trip to Transylvania for the royal wedding, Olivia had caught a floating rose head from the meadow. The Free Rose of Summer. Prince Alex had told her and Ivy all about it. It had drifted toward her on a summer breeze, and her fingers had closed around the blue petals. She knew what a blue rose meant, according to the vampire legends: *impossible love.*

Then, the first time that she and Jackson had spoken after her return to Franklin Grove, he was the one to admit what was staring them in the face.

"Perhaps we should do our own things for now," he'd said gently. Olivia had been bracing herself for heartbreak, but instead the only thing she felt was . . . regret. She felt sure they'd both be sorry about the chance that had passed them by, but what could she do in the face of his fame? What could either of them do? Their next visit together had been pushed back indefinitely. *So much for my fairy-tale ending,* she thought now. Then she gave herself a shake—Jackson would be waiting for a reply to his text.

"Any publicity is good publicity, right? ;)," she typed. The green bar slid across the screen on her phone. Sent! She held her breath.

Her phone pinged. "Har. Har."

At that, Olivia couldn't help but smile. "Thank you for asking, though," she added. Of course, she wished things with Jackson hadn't had to come to an end, but at least he was being nice. There had to be some silver lining.

Olivia's phone buzzed again and she quickly picked up, thinking it was another text from Jackson. Her heart fell when she saw it was her bio-dad—"Are you still coming over?"

Coming over? Shoot! Olivia thought, and checked her watch. *I'm late!*

She grabbed her new color-blocked tote bag and sprinted out of the house. *Phew.* She stopped for a moment on the sidewalk, resting her hands on her knees and trying to catch her breath. *I'm only one girl,* she thought, *and an exhausted one at that.* She had spent all day helping her mother tidy up and now she was hustling over to Charles's house to help him with some mysterious research project. She didn't like to say no to people, but didn't her parents realize she wasn't a machine? Fortunately, staying occupied did keep Olivia from dwelling on Jackson too much.

But why won't my bio-dad tell me what I'm researching for? He wouldn't let her in his study, where he was doing his work, and he refused to tell her why he wanted the information. All he did was sit Olivia down at a computer and occasionally pop his head out to ask her to look up random things on the Internet, like the climate in New Zealand or the quickest route through Australia by train from Melbourne to Sydney!

Because Ivy had stayed behind in Transylvania, Olivia was now doing the job of two daughters and, despite three years of practice on the cheerleading squad, Olivia had to admit that the double duty was taking a serious toll on both her pep and her perkiness. She was actually wearing a *gray* shift dress—a gray shift dress paired with a hot pink scarf, maybe, but still gray! If her mood was starting to creep into her fashion sense, Olivia knew she must be slipping into a serious funk . . . and fast. *I'll lay out my purple skinny jeans to wear tomorrow. That ought to help.*

Olivia didn't blame Ivy for going to the Academy. She knew that her sister needed to learn everything she could about her vampire identity. For a long time, Olivia hadn't known anything about her own heritage, so she understood how important these things were.

As she turned the corner onto Undertaker Hill, Ivy's street, a girl darted out from behind a neighbor's wall. Olivia bumped straight into her, forehead first. "Ooof!" Olivia stepped back, rubbing her head.

"Oh, I'm sorry," said the girl loudly, glancing around. She looked about Olivia's age. She wore flared jeans and a baggy, flower-powered blouse that Olivia couldn't quite decide whether she liked or not.

"Sorry about that," said Olivia. "My brain's a bit loopy today."

"That's okay." The girl adjusted the strap of her tasseled boho bag. "I'm Holly Turner. I think I recognize you from school." Holly's hair was long and strawberry blond. Her complexion was pale—not Ivy pale, but she was as fair-skinned as an actress in one of those Jane Austen movies Ivy refused to watch with Olivia at sleepovers.

"Franklin Grove?" asked Olivia, trying to think if she could place the girl. She knew pretty much everyone by now, but she couldn't remember ever seeing Holly there.

"Uh-huh." Holly toyed with the small but high-tech digital camera dangling around her neck. "My family moved here not too long ago. Actually, since I'm new here, I was wondering if you might want to go to Mister Smoothie with me and grab a Blueberry Beauty Boosting smoothie? I saw the menu as I was passing and it just sounds so exotic!"

"Hey! That's my favorite! You have great taste," Olivia said, laughing.

The other girl laughed, too. "Oh, I don't know about that. But I just love anything different or unusual—foods or places—or anything that's new to me! My mom says that's why I'd make a great journalist."

Olivia had almost forgotten there was some-where she needed to be—almost, but not quite. Suddenly, she remembered her promise to help her bio-dad. "Oh, it's too bad. Normally, I'd love to go for a smoothie, but right now I'm on my way to my dad's house."

"Oh." Holly's mouth twisted to the side. Olivia heard a hitch in her breath. "I'd love to meet your sister," she said hopefully. "I've heard she's really cool. Isn't she living in Transylvania right now? How amazing is that!"

Heard? Wow, did Ivy's reputation really reach all the way across the globe? It was either that, or someone had been filling this girl in since she moved to Franklin Grove.

"Very cool," Olivia said, crossing her fingers behind her back at her fib. *Being separated from my twin is so not cool at all. But I guess this girl doesn't want to hear about all that.* "Transylvania is a great place—very exotic. You'd probably love it just as much as Ivy! You kind of remind me of her. She's sort of alternative, too, but in a totally different way. My sister leans a bit Goth." Olivia held her fingers apart an inch. "But she totally pulls it off. Just like you and your sophisticated hippie outfit."

A faint blush spread over the creamy tint of Holly's cheeks. "Cool." Absentmindedly, Holly opened and closed the lens on her camera. "I mean, thanks."

"Are you into photography?" asked Olivia, pointing.

"Yeah, well, as I said, I want to be a journalist," Holly mumbled. "I don't have any real experience yet, but I'm working on it. An exclusive—that's what I need." Her eyes lit up as though she'd just had an idea. "Hey—" she began to say.

"No way!" Olivia clapped her hands together

and pressed them to her lips. "This is too freaky. My sister wants to be a writer, too." She wished she could tell Holly about her time with Ivy as guest reporters for *VAMP* magazine, but sadly that tidbit of information was top secret.

"Really?" Holly asked. "She could totally get an exclusive in Transylvania. All those vampires just waiting to be interviewed!"

Olivia felt a spark of alarm and forced her smile not to fade. "Vampires aren't real; you do know that, don't you?"

Holly smiled. "Of course! I was joking. But maybe your sister would sympathize with another would-be writer. Do you think she'd let me interview her about Transylvania? Could you ask next time you talk to her?" In her excitement, she'd edged so close that Olivia found herself backing away. Holly's forehead wrinkled. "But wait—if your sister is all the way in Europe, then why are you going to her dad's house? Don't you have the same dad? I mean, you're twins, aren't you?"

Olivia felt herself blushing. "It's, um, complicated," she said. She liked this girl, but there was no way she was getting into all of that! She didn't have time to come up with an explanation and, besides, any story she gave Holly would be a lie and Olivia tried to avoid those as much as possible. "I'm just helping him with something." Olivia sidestepped the issue. *That wasn't a lie. Not really!*

Holly hooked her thumbs through the belt loops of her jeans and shrugged. "Some other time, then?"

"Are you kidding? Absolutely!" Olivia hoped she wasn't overdoing it on the enthusiasm, but it was always nice to make new friends and Holly was almost like another Ivy, just a little less grumpy.

"See you later, then," Holly said.

"Sure thing," Olivia agreed, before turning to hurry up the sloping sidewalk, toward the top of the hill and the cul-de-sac where Ivy's house was located. When she looked back over her shoulder, Holly was still standing in the same spot, watching her. Olivia waved uncertainly. *She's probably just bored and lonely being the new girl in town,* Olivia thought, watching her finally scurry off.

She rang Mr. Vega's doorbell. A snippet from Mozart's *Requiem* boomed from a pipe organ inside. *Vampires and their classical music,* thought Olivia. *So old-school!*

The thick, Gothic door swung open and Charles popped his head out. "Hello, Olivia." His usually coiffed hair poked in all directions and his midnight blue shirt was uncharacteristically rumpled. *Did his iron break or something?* Olivia's bio-dad looked like he hadn't slept in his coffin for days.

"Dad!" Olivia made a show of scanning him from head to toe. "What on earth are you researching? You look . . . Well, let's put it this way . . . you don't look your usual suave self!" Normally, Charles was one of the most stylish men she knew. He could walk straight onto the cover of a men's fashion magazine, but now? *Not so much.*

He motioned her in and Olivia saw that the dining room table was completely covered in loose sheets of paper. "Never mind that," he said quickly. "Can you find out about Australian wild-life and the threats they pose to trav—"

Olivia slapped her hands to her cheeks. "Oh . . . my . . . goodness . . ." A thought had dawned in

Olivia's head. She pointed at him, grinning from ear to ear.

"No, no, no." He pulled his fingers through his hair. "It's not what you—"

Too late! "You were going to say 'travelers,' weren't you?" Olivia's eyes narrowed. "And why would you be thinking of going to Australia and New Zealand unless . . . unless . . . Could it be that you're planning . . . *a honeymoon*?!" Olivia jumped up and down, squealing.

"Shhhh, shhhh." Charles gestured with his hands as if to tell Olivia to take it down a notch, but she couldn't help it, and, besides, it wasn't like anyone was listening.

Olivia wiped a tear from the corner of her eye. "I'm so happy! You're marrying Lillian!" Lillian was a sophisticated vampire whom Charles had met when Olivia first walked the red carpet with Jackson. Not only was Lillian gracious and kind, she also had the most to-die-for accessories on the planet. *Romance plus a killer wardrobe—swoon!* Olivia pressed her lips together and flattened a palm over her heart.

If Charles had been capable of blushing, Olivia

thought he would have been pinker than her cotton candy lip gloss. "I haven't asked her yet," he told Olivia. "So it's not guaranteed."

Olivia tilted her head to the side and folded her arms across her chest. "I can't imagine why she would ever say no. You guys are totally in love. Have you told Ivy yet?"

"No." Charles slid his hands into his pockets. "I was sort of waiting for the right time to tell you two. But *someone*"—his eyebrows shot up—"decided to become an amateur sleuth all of a sudden." Olivia grinned sheepishly. "I want to make sure I have the perfect wedding and honeymoon lined up before popping the question."

Judging by the amount of running around we've done the past few days, I'm sure it'll be just that, Olivia thought, *but* . . . "There's one thing that makes me . . . well . . ." Olivia furrowed her brow, trying to decide on the right way to phrase what she had to say. "No, no, it's nothing." She shook her head. She shouldn't have said anything.

Charles's face fell. "What is it? What's wrong?"

"Um, well, maybe," she began to point out, trying to be extra gentle, "maybe Lillian might like to be involved in planning her own wedding?" She didn't want to hurt her bio-dad's feelings, but sometimes men didn't really grasp the importance of white veils, hundreds of lilies, and the right bride-and-groom cake toppers. "It is every girl's dream, after all," she finished.

Charles breathed a sigh of relief. "For a moment there, I thought it was going to be something really bad." He rested his hand on her shoulder. "Don't worry. Nothing is going to be booked until I've checked it with Lillian. I'm leaving the finer details all down to her judgment. For now, I just want to look into venues. Take the initiative. Carpe diem!" Olivia mentally cringed. Sometimes Charles and her adoptive dad weren't so different—they were both equally embarrassing in their own ways. "So what do you think?" he continued. "Are you still in? Can you look up how long it would take to sail down the Nile on a barge?"

"A barge down the Nile!" Olivia's jaw dropped open. "Lillian is going to die! But in a good way," she corrected herself before she could freak out her bio-dad even more.

"Not for many, many more centuries. She *is* a vampire, remember." Charles returned to the study while Olivia cleared a spot at the table, swooshing her finger across the computer's keypad to bring it to life.

Olivia typed, "barge trip down Nile" into the search engine. *This is going to be the wedding of the decade,* she thought. But then she remembered that she had just returned from the Vampire Royal Wedding in Transylvania, and that, *too*, had been fabulous. *I guess there's no reason why they can't both be utterly awe-inspiring affairs.* It did seem to be the vampire way.

Olivia scrolled through the list of websites. *Uh-oh.* Something popped into her head. *Who will I go to the wedding with?* Ivy had Brendan and, until recently, she would have had Jackson. *Do not think about Jackson,* Olivia commanded herself. Under no circumstances should she be dwelling on the J-word. *Our split was friendly. Neither of us got hurt. It's for the best and that is that.* Still, she was thankful she had her bio-dad's research project to keep her busy, even if it did bring up the occasional unwanted thought. Olivia set her mouth in a line and wrote down a list of tour company phone numbers for Charles to try in the morning.

★ 🦇 ★

By the time Olivia left Ivy's house, the sun had dropped in the sky and was washing the clouds in soft pinks, yellows, and oranges. *Not a bad color palette for a wedding,* thought Olivia, wishing she had her camera.

She fished a pair of sunglasses out of her purple tote bag. Her eyes were a little sore after so many hours staring at a computer screen. Not that she minded. Knowing exactly what Charles was up to actually made the research fun! She yawned, covering her mouth with the back of her hand. She was wiped out! It was only six o'clock, and already she couldn't wait to collapse into bed.

"Olivia!" She heard someone calling her name. She spun around and there was Brendan, Ivy's boyfriend. Olivia remembered when Ivy had been too nervous even to say hello to the dreamy vampire boy with the long hair and chiseled chin, but now they were totally in love with each other.

"Hey, Brendan!" She waved. He crossed the

street at superspeed, checking to make sure no one was around. *Vampires! Always using their superpowers even for the simplest things,* thought Olivia, smiling to herself.

"Talk to Ivy today?" Brendan asked, chewing on a snack bar that looked a lot like chocolate.

"Yeah." Olivia walked alongside Brendan, past the intersection of Undertaker Hill and Cemetery Lane. "But only for a minute. She had to run to dinner. Those time differences are killing us! What is that?" She poked at the bar.

Brendan held up the wrapper for her to see. "It's a Taurus Bar. For energy." He took another bite. "There was a stand giving them away in the mall. Want some?"

Olivia clutched her throat and pretended to gag. "Ugh, no thanks." She pushed it away. "It smells like stale cheese crackers. And what does a vampire need an energy bar for, anyway?"

Brendan shrugged, studying the shiny wrapper. "I don't know. Why do I care? Who turns down free food?"

Olivia rolled her eyes. "Not growing teen boys, I guess."

"Plus, it's high in calories," he said, reading. "And in glucosamine and oxymistine."

"Ummm . . ." Olivia glanced sideways at him. "Are you speaking English?"

"It's a synthetic ingredient that helps pump oxygen around the bloodstream. Great for giving an extra boost!" He thumped his chest with his fists.

Olivia giggled. "I'm not sure I want to see a vampire with extra energy!"

"I'm training to get as buff as possible before Ivy gets back. I want to impress her!" Brendan took the last chomp out of the Taurus Bar and strolled over to one of the Franklin Grove community garbage cans, where he tossed out the wrapper. He brushed his hands off, smiling a sad smile as he walked back over. "I really miss her, you know," he said, wiping his mouth. "Even though I'm super-excited she's getting to go on this whole adventure and everything." *Poor Brendan.* Olivia felt exactly the same.

"You know, you don't have to do anything to impress Ivy. She thinks you're totally cool just the way you are." Olivia took a hesitant step forward, wondering if she should give him a hug, but stopped herself. *I'm not sure I've ever hugged Brendan.* She let her arms fall to her sides. She wasn't sure how he'd react. As she pulled back, she noticed something. Brendan's neck and fore-arms were splotched all over with strange gray patches. Like some kind of weird zombie rash.

She remembered the horrible reaction she'd had to the Bloodbite Nettles she'd gotten tangled up in back in Transylvania. The vampire plant had made her skin red and bumpy, and it itched ten times worse than any case of the chicken pox. She hoped Brendan wasn't coming down with a weird variation of that. *Maybe he misses Ivy so much he's made himself lovesick—literally!*

"Brendan . . ." Olivia said, not taking her eyes off the gray blotches. "Are you feeling okay?"

Brendan cracked his neck and wiggled his fin-gers, shaking out his arms. "Yeah, I feel fine." He paused. "How have you been, since Ivy left?"

"Me? Well . . ." Olivia chewed her lip. "You know."

Brendan gave her a smile tinged with sadness. "Yeah, I know." The two of them gazed out across

Franklin Grove. It just wasn't the same without Ivy. Then Brendan cleared his throat. "Um, I like your . . . erm . . . outfit today, Olivia. Very, um, pretty."

"What are you talking about?" Olivia asked. Brendan was nice and everything, but she didn't think he'd ever noticed any outfit she'd put together until now. He looked at her hopefully. *Uh-oh*, she thought. *I smell a rat.*

"That's so sweet of you," she said, folding her arms and fixing on an overly bright smile. "What is it that you like in particular?" She swiveled around, as though to give him a better view of the ensemble.

She tried not to laugh as Brendan's eyes widened. He waved a hand in the direction of her tunic. "Um, the color. It's very . . . gray."

"Anything else?" Olivia prompted.

"And the . . . Your hair is . . ." He sighed. "Okay, you've got me."

"So what's the favor?" Olivia said, laughing. "You know, the one you're buttering me up for."

Brendan lowered his head and peered out from behind his shaggy hair, shifting his weight from one foot to the other. "Well, see, there is *one* thing." Olivia knew it! "Ivy forgot about something when she decided to stay behind in Transylvania."

"She forgot something?" Olivia repeated. "Like a toothbrush? Because I've seen that place, and I'm pretty sure she's all set. It's like she's going to school at the Ritz! They probably have a twenty-four-hour concierge service and everything."

"No, nothing like that. Ivy, Sophia, and I had made, um, *plans*," he said.

"Plans?" Olivia cocked her head.

"Yeah, and they're sort of the type of plans that *need* Ivy."

"Okay . . ." What kind of plans would the three vampire friends make? Blood drinking? A coffin slumber party? A crawly feeling began to spread up the back of Olivia's neck. She had a hunch that she wasn't going to like where this was going.

Brendan sighed. "When I tell you, you're going to freak out."

Uh-oh. Olivia felt another item being added to her to-do list—and if it was something that Brendan and ultra-Goth Ivy had cooked up together, it was bound to be something that would take her *totally* outside of her comfort zone. What was Brendan going to ask—and, more important, was Olivia ready to hear it?

CHAPTER 3

Transylvania vampires might not suck blood any-more, Ivy thought, *but I'm pretty sure they're about to suck the life right out of me.* Petra was seated in the desk next to her, doodling bats in a new black notebook. Ivy was dreading this class more than the *beep-beep-beep*ing of her morning alarm clock. *I don't even understand why I have to be steeped in vampire mythology and etiquette,* she thought, tapping her foot against the floor. Shc was a twenty-first-century girl, after all!

An uptight vampire sitting on Ivy's other side kept playing with her pearls, and it was driving Ivy batty.

"Hey, where are all the boys?" she asked out loud, looking around at the other students.

No sooner had the question escaped her mouth than every girl around her burst out laughing, including Petra.

"The boys?" exclaimed the girl with the strand of pearls. "You thought we would have class with boys?"

Ivy shrank back. "Sort of?"

Petra leaned over her desk. "Have you forgotten? I told you when you first came to Wallachia that boys and girls don't get to mix. We're completely segregated! We're not supposed to talk to them, and we never get to have class together." She sighed. "The only time we come halfway close to mingling is in Herbal Science and that's only because there's only one greenhouse available to the entire student body."

Ivy did remember now. When she'd been visiting the Academy to see what it was like, a duel had broken out on a playing field, and everyone had run out to watch. It had made Petra's day because they had gotten to be with the boys for a while. But it had only made Ivy feel uncomfortable, and she felt the same way now.

"Wow, how crazy!" she said. *There are some things I still can't believe about this place.*

The room went quiet again as they waited for their teacher to arrive.

"Pssssst!" Petra poked Ivy's arm with her pen. "Have you seen the Gauntlet yet?" she asked.

"No. Who's in that movie?" Ivy was asking when the door to the classroom was flung open and in flew a gigantic black bat, wings outstretched, with beady eyes and long, curved claws. Ivy ducked as it swooped over the heads of the students in the class. Girls screamed and scrambled under desks, while others pinned their bodies against the classroom walls, wailing. *Haven't they seen a bat before?* Ivy thought. It finally looped back to settle on the shoulder of a statuesque female vampire, who had slipped into the room unnoticed. She was wearing a mustard-colored, ruffle-necked blouse tucked into a ballooning hoop skirt, and her hair was slicked back into a ridiculously tight bun that pulled at the skin of her face.

The woman's got presence, Ivy admitted to herself, admiring the confident way the vampire strutted to the front of the classroom. *Even if her fashion sense does seem to be stuck in the nineteenth century.* The woman clapped her hands twice.

"Students," she said curtly, looking out at the rows of desks like she had lasers for eyeballs. "I am Miss Avisrova." The teacher bowed, and Ivy had to stop herself from snorting with laughter. The motion was so formal, so contrived. Was a simple *hello* not good enough? "As you all know, this is Vampire Etiquette. *Usually* we will be studying such crucial subjects as ballroom dancing, vampire cuisine, and the art of telling the difference between finely aged blood and the cheap stuff one would find at a BloodMart." Miss Avisrova sniffed the air as if she smelled something particularly foul. Ivy gulped. She had no idea that the BloodMart was considered so lowbrow. It was her favorite place to shop! "But today, as punishment for all the students who reacted in such an unseemly manner to the arrival of a bat"—Ivy shrank in her chair—"we will forgo the original lesson plan. I *was* going to teach you the correct way to behave at a formal ball." *Well, that's a relief,* thought Ivy, doing a mental eye roll. "Now, however, I will be instructing you in the subtle art of conversation."

Ugh. Miss Avisrova was so dour, so miserable-looking, *Miss* Depress*rova would be more fitting.* Was she playing some sort of character, like on a bad audition for *Transylvania's Got Talent*? If it weren't for the terror in the eyes of the students around her, Ivy would have believed this was all an elaborate practical joke.

"Miss Lazar," said Miss Avisrova. Ivy kept her head still, even though her instinct was to look around for the student in question. *How unlucky to be called on the very first day!* "Miss Lazar!" their teacher repeated. This time, Ivy couldn't help pivoting in her seat a little. *Lazar*—it might be a student she was related to, since that was her grandparents' last name. Ivy, of course, had the same last name that her father had adopted— Vega—but who was this other Lazar character? Maybe a cousin? The silence in the classroom rang in her ears.

Ivy turned her attention back to the front of the class to see that Miss Avisrova was staring straight at her. *Oh. Oops. Um* . . . Ivy had been about to shrug, but was shrugging allowed in etiquette class? She didn't think so. Miss Avisrova beckoned Ivy forward with one long, slender finger. Ivy's heart pounded like nails into a coffin lid. She slid out of her chair and walked up the long row of desks to the blackboard where Miss Avisrova was waiting.

"Sit down." The teacher snapped her fingers and pointed at a spare chair, which had been pushed up against the front wall. "Miss Lazar here will be my assistant," she told the class.

"It's *Miss Vega*, actually," said Ivy, fidgeting in her new seat. "Long story, pretty dull." Ivy tried to laugh but it came out fake and tinny. She pressed her lips together. *Yikes, stop talking, Ivy.* She tried to lift the corners of her mouth into a tight grin, but felt as if it probably better resembled a grimace. Ivy snuck a peek at the other students still sitting at their desks. Every one of them was staring at her like she'd just hurled an insult at the Queen of England! *How completely terrific.*

Avisrova tilted her head and looked at Ivy. "In conversation," she said, dragging a chair to sit opposite her, "one must never volunteer unsolicited personal information." *What does that even mean?* Ivy wondered. "Conversation is like a joust. To converse properly, you must probe at the other person. Never pry." Avisrova lifted her pinkie as if to punctuate this point. "You should ask carefully selected questions, to which you will receive carefully considered answers. Allow me to demonstrate." She straightened her back. "Miss Lazar, please *carefully* select a question for me, so that I may show you how a conversation should proceed."

Ivy chewed the side of her mouth, thinking. *Okay . . . how about, Why are you so odd? What makes your posture so straight? Are you against wearing shoes that don't look Victorian? Why in darkness' name does all this snooty vampire etiquette matter?* Ivy pushed back the questions floating in her mind. They were sure to get her into trouble. *Choose carefully.*

Ivy took a deep breath. "What's your favorite TV show?" *Everyone* had to have a favorite television show, didn't they?

Avisrova scoffed, shaking her head. "How *American* of you," she told Ivy. "Such a trivial, meaningless question. Why would you even bother to ask it?"

Anger flared up bright and hot in Ivy's chest. She heard whispers coming from around the room, and Ivy shot one of the girls the evil eye. The girl jumped and sat up straighter in her chair, making a show of smoothing the pleated skirt of her uniform.

"Can you believe she said that?" said another girl, whose hair was plaited into soft braids that fell over each side of her collarbone.

"So uncivilized," commented another, who was wearing a crimson ribbon as a headband. *Kristina? Anna?*—Ivy couldn't remember the girl's name and, right now, she barely cared.

Ivy's nails bit into her palms. She cleared her throat. "I mean," she began, feeling a slight snarl creep into the edge of her voice, "what's it like shopping in the 1960s?"

There was a collective gasp. *Fine,* Ivy knew the insult hadn't *entirely* made sense. After all, Avisrova wasn't dressed as a hippie. But Ivy had made her point, and the astonished reaction coming from her classmates was totally worth it—she hoped.

Avisrova shot her a death stare that would have

taken Ivy herself years to master. "You will be punished for that," she barked. "But don't worry. This school will train the insolent American ways right out of you, Ivy *Lazar*." Miss Avisrova glared down her nose at her. "You will report to me at the end of the day. I will be very surprised if either of us gets any dinner tonight."

Before Ivy could stop herself, she blurted out, "What is this, *Oliver Twist*?"

Loud scoffs sounded around the room and Ivy caught more than a few sneers on the faces of her classmates. She sighed. *Today is not off to a good start.*

★ 🦇 ★

"Oh my darkness, and then you were all like, 'What is this, *Oliver Twist*?'"

Ivy groaned. Petra was skipping beside her after class, quoting back Ivy's run-in with Miss Avisrova for the umpteenth time. They passed the trophy case filled with polished bronze medals, plaques, and trophies, awarded for everything from rugby to fencing to spelling bees.

"I know. I was there," Ivy reminded Petra.

A girl with a red and black headband and silky

brown hair patted her on the back. "Nice job, Ivy." She flashed a grin.

Another student with glitzy diamond stud earrings and a fitted blazer came up and shook Ivy's hand in the hall. "I have to say, you're pretty brave—if a little crazy."

Ivy bit back a laugh. She didn't want to offend anyone, but if they thought *that* was reckless, these girls wouldn't last a day at Franklin Grove Middle School. *And that's just an ordinary, run-of-the-mill suburban school!*

Ivy was about to say as much when she saw Petra peering starry-eyed through the open door of a classroom. Ivy followed her gaze to where a crowd of boys, all dressed in crisp black blazers and red ties, was sitting on desks and tossing paper airplanes at one another before class.

"What are you—"

"Come here!" Petra pulled Ivy away from her new fan club and into an alcove at the end of the hall. "Check it out," she said, digging her notebook out of a leather cross-body satchel. Petra flipped through a few pages before folding back half the notebook and holding it up for Ivy to see.

Inside, Petra had doodled a picture of a boy and a girl perched side by side on a coffin while holding hands. In curly script, she'd labeled the girl "Me" and the boy "Etan." Hearts wrapped around the border of the drawing, colored in with red ink. *Petra must have a serious crush!*

"Cool sketches," said Ivy, running her fingers over the page.

"That's not all. The best bit is the poem," Petra explained, turning the page. Ivy scanned the lines of writing, catching words like *burning, passion,* and *darling. A love poem?* Ivy thought. It seemed a little cheesy to her. "I've never been able to write my poetry in class before." Petra hugged the notebook to her chest. "The teachers are always way too eagle-eyed. But while you were keeping Avisrova occupied in the lesson today, I got to pen this! I'm sticking close to you!" She squeezed Ivy's arm.

"Um . . . thanks?" said Ivy. She was glad she could help Petra, but she hadn't planned on annoying a teacher so quickly after arriving at the Academy, and she wasn't sure she cared much about giving Petra opportunities to write silly love poems. *Still,* she thought, *at least someone can see a bright side to me getting detention!*

Petra stuffed her notebook back in her satchel and pulled out her phone to check the time. "We've got five minutes until class. We better get going."

Together, they stepped outside onto the lush Wallachia grounds. The grass sparkled with dew and Ivy took a deep breath, enjoying the aroma of the gardenia bushes that lined the stone walkway. All around them, young vampire students were lounging under shady oak trees, propped up against the trunks reading textbooks. Others were running around the lawn tossing Frisbees. The scene looked like something out of one of those teen prep-school dramas Olivia watched on TV.

Petra and Ivy headed toward the school hall, where choir practice was due to start.

"See that over there?" asked Petra. "That's the Gauntlet." Petra pointed at a hill that sloped away from the girls' dormitory before ending in a dense forest, filled with tall pines and broad-leaved evergreens. Poison ivy climbed up tree trunks, and red berries hung heavily from bushes. The forest floor was dense with leaves, and nasty patches of nettles squatted at the bases of tree trunks, waiting to sting anyone walking past.

Ivy stopped walking, cupping her hand over her eyes to shield them from the sun. "What's a gauntlet?"

"*The* Gauntlet," Petra corrected her. "It's what Wallachia Academy uses to keep girls and boys apart outside of lesson time. Haven't you noticed that the only time we see the boys is when they're on their way back to their dorm rooms or from their lessons? The Gauntlet is what separates our living quarters."

The forest was dark and thick. Ivy didn't know how someone could see more than two inches in front of their face in there, much less sneak through for a romantic meeting. *The school board at Wallachia Academy really doesn't want the girls and boys mixing!* Ivy thought. What was the problem? If she'd been kept apart from Brendan like that back in Franklin Grove . . . Ivy shuddered. She didn't want to think about it. She might have been hundreds of miles away from her boyfriend right at that moment, but she knew they'd be reunited one day soon—and there wouldn't be any stupid Gauntlet to keep them apart.

Petra shook her head, staring out over the trees. "If only there wasn't this stupid forest in the way." She gave a deep sigh. "Etan lives right over there. I wonder what he eats for breakfast. . . ."

Ivy glanced sideways at Petra. She could swear she saw the glisten of tears in her eyes. *Oh, please.* Then Petra looked at her hopefully.

"Of course, with you here, anything could happen now. Just think! One day I might even get to have an actual conversation with Etan. You know, if you keep the teachers distracted."

Hold it right there! Ivy thought. Was Petra hanging around her only because she thought Ivy's talent for trouble would provide a good cover for her? *Hello! I'm not a human decoy!* Or was she genuinely opening up to Ivy? Petra seemed so confident most of the time; Ivy was sure she wouldn't talk to most of the other students like this.

Ivy sighed. One nice thing about Franklin Grove—the people were a lot less complicated. *I almost wish I was back there. . . . I wonder what Brendan's doing right now?* Just thinking this made her feel a little more sorry for Petra. It hurt Ivy to be so far from her boyfriend, and it must really hurt Petra to know that the boy she liked was just on the other side of this forest.

"I have an idea," Ivy said, walking over to inspect one of the trees on the edge of the Gauntlet. *It looks sturdy enough—surely it can take two girls scrambling up into its branches. . . .* "Shall we?" she asked, turning back to her friend.

"Shall we what?" asked Petra.

"Shall we take a peek?" Ivy patted the thick tree trunk.

Petra looked from Ivy to the tree and back to Ivy. "You've got to be kidding me! We can't." Petra shook her head rapidly. "I can't."

"Etan might be over there." Ivy smiled innocently. "Besides, we have a couple minutes to kill, don't we?"

Petra set her jaw, practically glaring at the tree. "You're right. I have to see him. Give me a boost."

Ivy held out her hands, lacing her fingers together to form a step for Petra like she had seen her sister do during cheerleading practice. She lifted Petra to the lowest branch, and in turn Petra reached out a hand to help Ivy up. Together, they scrambled to a higher branch.

"Can you see them?" Ivy asked, breathing hard.

Petra pointed. "There, on the field. There's a bunch of boys playing." Ivy watched them running around in their soccer jerseys, waiting for the game to start.

"This is crazy," Ivy laughed, even though she wasn't sure she really thought it was funny. "It's like we're living at a zoo and the boys are the main exhibit."

Petra clutched her heart. "I wish we had better views, then. Up close and personal."

This girl has it bad! "Yeah," Ivy said, leaning back against the trunk, her legs dangling from the branch she was sitting on. "Back in Franklin Grove I got to hang out with my boyfriend all the time. He was one of my best friends. I can't imagine . . . living like this."

The two of them were quiet. Beside her, Ivy could sense Petra holding her breath, probably hoping for a glance of Etan.

There was the sound of a twig snapping, and an adult's voice called from the base of the tree.

"You two, what are you doing up there?" A long-nosed teacher with circular glasses peered up at them from below.

Ivy and Petra looked at each other wide-eyed and scrambled down.

"Coming!" called Ivy.

She dropped to the ground only a moment after Petra and brushed off her uniform.

"Sorry, Miss . . . um . . ."

"Kornikova," said the woman, like she'd just swallowed a spoonful of curdled milk.

"Miss Kornikova. Right." Ivy tried to look innocent. "You see, we were just preparing for our first Herbal Science class this afternoon and— Oh, look at the time! We better get going!"

Ivy grabbed Petra's hand and the two of them scurried away, walking fast past the forest. Petra had fallen silent again, and Ivy was glad to be left to her own thoughts for a few moments. *That was a close call!*

The two of them sat through lessons that felt more like torture for Ivy: Potion Mixing that involved slimy frog parts, and then on to Fang Maintenance, where they were taught the finer points of making steak tartare. Ivy loved Gothic songs, but her newly long fangs kept catching on her gums. And although she loved eating steak tartare, she hated chopping up the meat with the raw egg! *Where's Horatio when you need him?*

Soon, it was finally time for Herbal Science. They headed toward a large, glass greenhouse. This was one class that Ivy was actually looking forward to. Around the time of Prince Alex and Tessa's royal wedding, Ivy had discovered her knack for vampire botany. Olivia had been mistakenly treated with vampire medicine after she'd fallen into a nasty patch of Bloodbite Nettles, and, with the help of the Lazar family herbal scientist, Helga, Ivy had created a new poultice, mixing plants and potions to cure her twin sister.

They arrived outside the state-of-the-art greenhouse with its whirring fans and electric sprinklers. Half a dozen metal tables were set up behind a chalkboard, with stools lined up along both sides of the tables. Potted plants hung from above, their tendrils snaking through the air.

"Good afternoon, class!" From behind a

screen, an older vampire woman emerged, wearing a dark green apron and canvas gloves. Her frizzy gray hair was pulled back into a messy ponytail and she had streaks of dirt covering both cheeks.

"Helga?" Ivy blurted before she could stop herself. Helga was the Lazar family's gardener, who had inspired Ivy's interest in the subject during the wedding! "I didn't know you were teaching here."

"Ivy Vega!" Helga peeled off her gloves and rushed over to Ivy, hand extended. Ivy was about to pull Helga to her in a hug, when she noticed something sparkling on her ring finger. Ivy froze, staring at Helga's hand. It was an antique diamond ring. "You're engaged!" she exclaimed.

Helga gave Ivy a shy smile. "Horatio proposed yesterday. We decided we didn't have any time to waste!" Olivia and Ivy had witnessed the butler's crush on Helga develop into full-blown love during the preparation for the royal wedding. Olivia had thought it was the most romantic thing ever, and even Ivy had to admit she was pleased to see these two amazing people sharing secret glances.

It had been like watching two old-style Hollywood actors politely charm each other in one of those black-and-white movies that were shown on rainy Saturday afternoons.

"Really? That's killer!" This time she did pull Helga in for a heartfelt hug.

"Do they know each other?" Ivy heard one of the other students ask. "I thought she came from some dorksville place called Franklin Grove."

Helga pulled away, flattening her hair back into place. "Um, class?" she said, returning to the front of the room. "I'm sure you are wondering what I am doing here. Miss Petrovsky had a sudden change of heart. She decided to retire. Something about allergies and children and a bad case of the sucker-footed bat pox. Anyway, please allow me to introduce myself. The Academy would like you to call me Miss Peneve, but"—she glanced over her shoulder—"I would like you to call me Helga."

Ivy took her place at one of the desks. Petra was watching, her brow creased in a frown, as though she was annoyed to see Ivy with a friend from the past. But nothing could spoil Ivy's delight at seeing Helga and remembering the good times they'd spent together, mixing potions.

Maybe good things can happen at Wallachia, after all, she thought. Things were definitely looking up.

CHAPTER 4

Deep breaths, Olivia, deep breaths, she told herself. *We're twins, remember? Identical twins.*

Olivia's palms were sweating and she kept jiggling her right knee. She was totally going to give it away—especially if the layers of Goth makeup she had painted on started dripping off her face. *I have to calm down.* She'd pulled off looking like Ivy before, and she could do it again—couldn't she?

She was standing in line at the box office that was set up in Franklin Fields. Sophia and Brendan stood waiting in line with her, among all the superfans clad in band T-shirts. Brendan was bouncing up and down on the balls of his feet, looking both nervous and excited. He pulled his hands out of his jacket and gave her a thumbs-up and a sly smile that was probably supposed to be encouraging, but came out as more Dracula-style sinister. "You're going to be fine!" He thumped her on the back.

"Really?" she asked. She wasn't quite so sure. She'd done her best to research Ivy's favorite band, looking at fan sites on the Internet, but would she really manage to fool everyone into thinking that she was the rightful owner of the tickets Ivy had won? "Are you sure I'm doing . . . okay?"

"Totally," Sophia reassured her with an arm squeeze.

I'm actually pulling this off! She only felt a little bit bad about the fibs that she'd have to tell in order to help Brendan. Look how pumped he and Sophia were to be here! Their happiness had to offset at least some of her guilt, didn't it?

Olivia couldn't believe it when Brendan had eventually explained the favor that he needed from her. Two weeks before she and Ivy had left for Transylvania, Ivy had entered her name into a competition for three VIP passes to see the Pall Bearers, her absolute favorite angry metal band. Ivy had won the tickets—Brendan had been copied in on the e-mail, as he was listed as an invitee Ivy would bring with her—but now she wasn't around to claim them! Of course Olivia had ended up agreeing to help. She couldn't leave Brendan and Sophia in the lurch.

"I can't believe we're actually here!" Brendan said now, pumping his fist. "Who would have thought Ivy would actually win?"

Olivia wished that Brendan would hold off celebrating until they were in the clear. She hadn't actually picked the tickets up yet. "I'm just sorry Ivy can't be here," Olivia said weakly. *Seriously. You have no idea how much I wish my twin were here instead of me.* "Missing all this? She's going to feel like she's been staked!"

"She had a lot on her mind," said Sophia. "It's understandable that she forgot that she entered the competition." Both she and Brendan had been completely understanding, but this was the Pall Bearers they were talking about. When news came out about the tickets, what were they supposed to do? Miss out on the greatest band ever? Olivia knew Ivy would feel terrible if her decision to attend Wallachia had kept her friends from enjoying the event of a lifetime. So, here she was, trying to do the best, most convincing Ivy impression she had ever done. Her Hollywood life might be on hold, but that didn't stop Olivia from acting her socks off!

Olivia tugged at the baggy black T-shirt she was wearing—so not her style—but Sophia and Brendan could only get tickets if the winner, a certain "Ivy Vega," claimed them personally, and the man at the box office had Ivy's photo on file from her original application. Olivia took another step forward in line. It was almost her turn.

"We'd better cut out," said Brendan, ducking under the velvet ropes and out of line.

"Good luck," whispered Sophia in her ear.

Olivia pulled a compact out of the pocket of her torn jeans. She studied her reflection. *Black wig? Check. Pale makeup? Check. Grungy clothes that may or may not need to go in the laundry? Check, check, check.*

Now only three people separated her from the front of the line. Olivia refused to sneak another look over at Brendan and Sophia. *Just keep calm and you'll get through it. It will be fine.*

"What was the first Pall Bearers song to top the Transylvania Billboard Charts?" she overheard the bearded man working inside the box office ask the teenager standing first in line.

In order to redeem their prize, each winner had to answer a trivia question about the band to prove their fandom. Even though it was a warm evening, a spike of cold went through Olivia's heart.

"'Welcome to My Frightmare'!" the winner answered enthusiastically.

"That is . . . correct!" The box office man handed over the tickets. "Next!"

Olivia was shivering with nerves. Sophia had spent all day helping Olivia study, but what if they asked something Olivia didn't know? Come to think of it, Olivia wasn't sure she could remember anything!

Olivia stared blankly at the back of the head of the person in front of her as the bearded man asked, "What is the lead singer's cat's name?"

Olivia felt as though someone had shaken her brain and erased it like an Etch A Sketch.

"Zombie Gray!" answered the girl, who was wearing fishnet stockings and knee-high boots. She took her tickets and waved them around.

It was Olivia's turn. She shuffled forward as if on autopilot.

"Name?" the man asked, scratching his beard and looking bored.

Olivia squared her shoulders. "Ivy Vega."

He rifled through his list of winners. "Vega . . . Vega . . . Ah, here you are." He looked from the picture to Olivia and back at the picture again. Olivia held her breath. "Right," he continued. "Your question is: What is the third line in the second song on the first album?"

Say what!? This was definitely not something they had studied. Olivia felt herself go whiter than the shade of Pale Beauty makeup she was wearing. How was she going to wing *this*?

Eyes wide, she looked over at Brendan and Sophia, who had already begun performing a ridiculous game of charades. Olivia squinted. She knew they were trying to tell her the answer, but what on earth were they miming?

Sophia was furiously tapping her chest with one hand and pointing at Brendan with the other, while Brendan had brought his fingertips together in a sharp point and was making swift prodding motions into the air.

Chest? No. Heart? Love . . . thumping . . . pointy thing . . . crying?

Olivia shook her head, turning back to the man at the box office, who was now reading the sports pages, waiting for Olivia to respond. *Might as well give it a try,* she thought.

"'This love is like a stake through the heart'?" she said.

He peeled his eyes away from the newspaper to read the answer sheet. "Here you go," he said, sliding three tickets toward her. Olivia snatched them. *Seriously? I did it?* She wanted to jump for joy, but she was pretty sure Goths weren't allowed to show that much enthusiasm about anything. Instead, she walked coolly over to Brendan and

Sophia, wondering: *Who would listen to a song about love and stakes?*

* 🐰 *

Half an hour later, Olivia was busy avoiding getting her toes crushed underneath combat boots in a sea of Goth girls and guys, who were all so ghostly pale it almost looked as if they'd drained the color from the usually vibrant park. The three of them scoped out a spot on the grass and spread a blanket among the other concert goers, who all sat in clusters, waiting for the gig to start.

"This"—Sophia stared up at the blazing spotlights—"is killer." They were sprawled out in the winner's enclosure right beneath the stage, and even Olivia had to admit it was pretty cool. She had never been this close to see a band play live.

"You ready to hear your new favorite song?" Brendan nudged Olivia playfully.

She dropped her chin. "Any song that compares love to being staked will not be playing on my iPod!"

The lights dimmed and a roar rose up from the crowd. Brendan pulled Olivia to her feet just before the crowd surged forward. The place was a madhouse! She clung to Brendan's hand so as not to be crushed. *Pall Bearer fans are rabid.*

"Brendan!" Olivia yelled, still clutching onto him. His hand was scalding hot, like he had a hundred-and-ten-degree fever. "Are you okay?" she asked.

"Yeah, yeah," he said, letting go. "I'm fine."

Olivia peered up at Ivy's boyfriend. She couldn't put her finger on why, but she didn't think Brendan was telling the truth. He looked hot and flustered. *Something's definitely wrong.* Before she could ask any more questions, music blasted from the speakers and amps situated at the end of the stage. How could vampires stand this? They had super-sensitive hearing, but Olivia could barely handle it and she was human! It was the single loudest noise Olivia had ever heard. She would have plugged her ears if only her arms weren't pinned to her sides in the crowd. Now all she could do was cringe. She felt like her parents—*Turn the music down!*

Sophia bounced next to her, pumping her fist to the pounding drumbeat. A red light illuminated the stage, revealing the Pall Bearers, dressed in skinny jeans and ripped T-shirts. The lead guitarist jammed on the strings of his instrument, and what came out was a tuneless, rhythmless mess.

Fright Night, nocturnal delight
Turn out the light and
Scream with all your might . . .

Olivia had nothing against Goths, but they had terrible taste in music. *This could not possibly get any worse. . . .* Or at least that was what Olivia thought before the dancing started. If it could even be called *dancing*. The crowd surged one way and then the other, like an angry, writhing snake, and Olivia was wrenched along in the current.

"Ouch!" Someone stomped on her toe. "Oof!" An elbow jabbed into her back and she lurched forward. When she regained her balance, she tried standing on her tiptoes so that she could just see over the shoulders of the people directly in front of her. There was a little clearing within the mass of people, in which a bunch of rowdy boys were shoving and kicking one another, yelling, "Mosh,

mosh, mosh, mosh!" *This is supposed to be fun?*

There was a brief lull between the first and second songs, and Olivia jumped at the opportunity to talk to Sophia. "Mind if I head out now?" She tugged at the sleeve of Sophia's faded Pall Bearers shirt. "I'm not sure I feel like being deaf tomorrow." Already her ears were ringing.

Sophia wrapped Olivia in a tight hug. "Thank you so, so much for coming through for us. I was beyond excited for this concert. You have no idea."

Despite her full-body discomfort, Olivia couldn't help but smile. So what if she had to suffer a few bruised ribs and a little hearing loss? *Totally worth it. If only Ivy could be here . . .*

Olivia hadn't started to make her escape yet when the lead singer came to the front of the stage with the microphone. "For this next song, we'll need a volunteer backup singer."

A million cries of "Pick me, pick me!" sounded from all around the crowd. One thing was for sure: Olivia was not among them. She looked over her shoulder. The singer was a handsome but wiry Goth guy, wearing a dragon-design

T-shirt—*Or, wait!* Olivia looked closer. *Perhaps it's one massive tattoo!*

"We've picked one person at random from among our lucky competition winners." He unfolded a piece of paper and waved it over his head. "Where is Ivy Vega?"

Olivia stopped dead, her jaw dropping open. *No. Way.*

"Why did we ever think I would be able to pull this off without getting into some kind of weird trouble?" she hissed to Brendan. Sophia's eyebrows shot up and she slapped her hands to her cheeks.

"So sorry," Sophia mouthed.

Why am I even surprised? Olivia thought. Every single time she and Ivy switched places, it caused some sort of craziness. *You name it, I've had it.*

Before Olivia knew what was happening, she was being hoisted onto the shoulders of the rabid Pall Bearers fans. She had a brief flash of the moment when her classmates at Franklin Grove paraded her around the gym after the school dance she'd planned. But the memory came to an abrupt halt when Olivia was tipped on her back and crowd-surfed all the way to the stage.

She stumbled to her feet, forced upright by the sheer power of the crowd behind her. Olivia stared out at the ocean of black. The sight of the churning, surging fans gave her a strange, queasy feeling in the pit of her stomach, almost like vertigo. The stage lights beat down on her with white-hot heat.

From stage right, she noticed a roadie approaching her . . . with a microphone! *The horror!* Olivia started to panic. She numbly took hold of it. This could not be happening to her. The thought of karaoke was terrifying, and this was a hundred times worse. She spotted Brendan and Sophia at the foot of the stage, their mouths open in shock.

The lead singer—*what's his name again?*—made the devil's horn gesture to her with his fingers sticking up behind his ears. Not knowing what else to do, Olivia returned it.

"Right on!" he said, performing a high-flying jump and stamping down on the stage. "Now, I'm sure Ivy knows what to do," the singer told the crowd. "But just in case she's a little nervous, why don't we help her out by reminding her how the chorus goes." Olivia wiped the sweat off her forehead, wishing she had a paper bag to hyper-ventilate into. "When I say 'I,' you say"—he held the microphone out to the crowd—"'Hate You!'"

"Got it." Olivia nodded.

Ivy's vampire education had better be worth it, she thought. *Because next time I see her, she is going to have to use everything she's learned to make this up to me!*

CHAPTER 5

I wonder what Olivia is doing right now?

Ivy had suffered in silence through three full days of classes, and Miss Avisrova had still managed to pick on everything Ivy had done in Etiquette class. Ivy used the wrong toothpick on her fangs. Ivy didn't know which side of the plate her blood goblet should be on. Ivy had no clue how to waltz to the Vampire Sonata!

But really, could learning the correct vampire etiquette take a *whole school year*? Luckily, Ivy had other classes that Avisrova didn't teach. She never thought she'd be so thankful for Potion Mixing, but at least it gave her a break.

The biggest bright spot was still, by far, Herbal Science. Every day, Ivy looked forward to her trek out to the greenhouse. For instance, yesterday, Helga had taught them how to cultivate herbs properly. With Petra as her lab partner, Ivy had helped plant, water, and fertilize a variety of herbs, some familiar and others vamp-exotic—like the Fang Fennel with its spiky stalks that made a biting motion if a hand came too close.

Today, Herbal Science was the second class of the day. Ivy arrived carrying a steaming travel mug filled with hot plasma tea, scooted out her stool from under a table on the girls' side of the room, and plopped herself down.

Herbal Science was the only class Ivy had where boys and girls were taught in the same classroom. Otherwise they were kept so segregated that Ivy thought the Wallachia staff might believe that it was still possible for students to catch the plague from one another. Even now they were divided by a long table running down the center of the greenhouse, and the height of the seemingly hundreds of potted plants made it nearly impossible for the boys and girls to see one another. Ivy hadn't even realized there *were* guys in the class the first day!

Helga clapped her hands to get the students' attention. She was standing on top of a tall podium so that she could look down on both sides of the classroom at once—the boys' side and the girls' side. *Helga's really growing into a great teacher,* thought Ivy. A miniature rake stuck out of the front pockets of Helga's apron. Her engagement ring flashed in the beams of natural light shining through the greenhouse windows.

"Everyone, for today's lesson, first I'll be showing you the correct way to extract certain types of herbs from the ground so as not to lose their potency, and then I'll let you try doing it. Sound good?"

This was more like it for Ivy—actually *doing* things. She'd never have thought that she would enjoy using gardening tools and wearing those stinky gloves, but she did. It beat stuffy Etiquette class any day.

After Helga had demonstrated gently digging out the roots of a Caped Parsley plant, Ivy retrieved a set of gardening tools from the supply closet and spread them out on the table.

Petra selected a hand trowel and poked Ivy with it.

"Ouch!" Ivy yelped, rubbing the spot on her arm. "What was that for?"

Petra bent over their potted plant and spoke out of the side of her mouth. "What is your deal?" she asked. "Why aren't you doing anything?" Petra glanced up at Helga, who was busy explaining to a student that she couldn't just slice through any roots that weren't cooperating.

"What do you mean?" said Ivy, grabbing a small shovel. "We haven't started yet."

"Not the stupid plant." Petra blew her fringe out of her face. "You're not talking back to the teacher. You're not getting into trouble. You haven't done anything Ivy-ish at all!"

Ivy noticed Petra trying to glance through the potted plant divider to the boys' side of the room. "I like Helga," Ivy reminded Petra. "I don't want to annoy her." She pushed at the plastic pot to loosen the dirt around their parsley.

"You're supposed to be creating a distraction," Petra whispered back. "I have to create my art when inspiration strikes, Ivy! And I'm so close to my Etan. Please!"

"No," said Ivy, scooping up a heap of soil. "I'm supposed to be extracting this herb, *not* creating a distraction."

What kind of poem or drawing can Petra be doodling in a greenhouse, anyway? And why can't she do it in her own time? Ivy looked around and all of a sudden Helga was standing behind them.

"Petra, Petra, Petra," Helga chided. "Did you really think you could whisper and not be heard? Or have you forgotten about a little thing called *vampire hearing*?" Petra shrank in her seat. *I guess she doesn't like being the one in trouble as much as she likes encouraging* other people *to get into it,* thought Ivy. "Do you girls need help with anything?" Helga asked.

Ivy carefully pulled out one of the sections of the plant's roots. "Nope. I think I've got it under control." She glanced over her shoulder. "What is this particular herb used for?"

"Caped Parsley?" Helga pinched the stem. "Well, its scientific name is Oxynamon. And it's used in a remedy to cure vampiric infections by increasing oxygen to the bloodstream. It can certainly come in handy in a crisis." Helga winked. She leaned in closer to Ivy and lowered her voice. "Who knows when any of us will find ourselves in a sticky situation? Knowledge and strength— they're a person's most important assets."

"But which name will be on the test? How will I get an A on my paper if I don't know whether to study the Latin name or the informal name?" whined Petra.

"Either will be acceptable." Helga heaved a sigh and turned away to leave, muttering under her breath, "So preoccupied with grades . . ." Ivy noticed a glint on Helga's wrist.

"Is that new?" asked Ivy, pointing to a silver bracelet. Between her and Olivia, Ivy was definitely not the fashionista of the pair, but she did know that Helga had not been wearing that bracelet the day before.

Helga pressed her thin lips together and made a big show of checking her watch. "Oh, is it that time already?"

"Oooooh, is that from a certain handsome butler?" Ivy teased. "Horatio, perhaps?"

Staring down her nose at Ivy, Helga gave her best stern-teacher look. "Perhaps," she said, her mouth twitching as she tried not to smile.

When Ivy turned her attention back to the table, she saw that Petra had maneuvered one of the potted plants an inch to the left, to make a small gap in the jungle that sat atop the dividing table. Petra had her elbows on the desk, her chin resting on her fists as she stared longingly at a handsome vampire boy on the other side. Was he the subject of her gushy love poems? He had wavy blond hair and sharp green-and-yellow eyes that gazed wistfully back at Petra. Was that Etan?

Ivy snuck glances at the two lovebirds, both of whom seemed to have completely forgotten there was anything going on outside of their little staring contest. *Maybe I was too hard on Petra,* Ivy thought. The poor girl was clearly lovesick, and the longing looks were as close as this couple was going to get to a relationship at Wallachia. *Star-crossed lovers!* Ivy could picture her sister mooning over the impossible romance. *I wonder if there is anything I can do to help Petra, after all.* Ivy knew that was what Olivia would want her to do.

Leave it with me, sis, Ivy thought. The queen of romance, aka Ivy's twin sister, may not have been at Wallachia Academy, but Ivy would try her best in Olivia's absence. How hard could it be, bringing two lovebirds together? What could possibly go wrong?

* 🦇 *

After class, Ivy was making her way across the grounds, feeling thankful for her special ultra-protective vampire contacts since the sun was already beating down full force. As she walked toward the cafeteria, she cast a quick look in the direction of the Gauntlet.

"Would you cross the Gauntlet for a boy?" a girl named Stacia was asking as she walked by with a classmate.

"No way," said her friend emphatically. "Have you heard? There are supposed to be hidden pits in there with snakes, waiting for a victim to fall in! And the Gauntlet Ghost can scare a person to death before they even have a chance to cry for help."

Ivy glanced over at the edge of the wood. It did look pretty spooky—haunted, even.

The girls were still talking. "Someone told me

that a female student went in there once, and when she came out, her hair had gone white from shock!"

The two of them laughed nervously. *Just a bunch of silly stories,* Ivy told herself, as she wandered farther ahead with Petra. But still, she felt a shiver pass over her. Entering the Gauntlet wasn't for the fainthearted, even if the stories were made up and all you were risking was getting a nasty rash from the berries and ivy.

Petra held open a heavy antique door for Ivy and they entered the main building. It was lunchtime, and after that they had Coffin Carpentry, which would mean Ivy got to go at least half the day without seeing Miss Avisrova.

But as Ivy strolled down the school hallway, she suddenly caught sight of a figure skulking beside a suit of armor. Ivy nearly shrieked. It was Miss Avisrova, standing completely still. She glowered at Ivy, following her with her eyes like one of those creepy portraits in a horror movie. *What is her problem?* Ivy didn't understand how or why the teacher was keeping such close tabs on her. *Doesn't she have anything else to do—like organize extracurricular classes in extreme pain?*

Ivy tugged Petra along. "Come on."

Petra stumbled behind her, watching with puppy-dog eyes as the boys walked back to their side of the grounds. "I love you," Petra mouthed at the retreating back of Etan, tracing a heart in the air.

Ivy groaned, rolling her eyes. "Okay, okay, stop being so dramatic."

Ivy didn't get a chance to dwell on her strange professor or on Petra's boy-craziness, though, because suddenly she was too busy wondering why her classmates were all staring at her as if they were completely starstruck.

"Petra, do I have something in my teeth?" Ivy bared her fangs for Petra to check. She'd been letting them grow back ever since entering the Academy. Usually, vampires in Franklin Grove were meticulous about filing their fangs back so that normal humans wouldn't notice anything odd. Here, fangs were the norm, and Ivy was quite enjoying the sensation of those sharp little teeth on either side of her mouth.

"No." Petra giggled for the first time all day.

There was a smattering of applause as Ivy passed. Some girls even mimed bowing and worshipping at her feet. *What is going on?* Ivy wondered. *My run-in with Miss Avisrova should be yesterday's news by now.*

A slender vampire with trendy blunt-cut bangs bounced over to Ivy with a notebook and a black marker. "Can I have your autograph?" she asked. "Make it out to Anastasia."

Ivy scribbled something unintelligible in the notebook. *Somewhere between Herbal Science and lunch I must have entered the Twilight Zone,* she thought.

"Am I being pranked?" Ivy ducked into the cafeteria with Petra and they grabbed a couple of seats at an empty table. Ivy arranged her chair so that she didn't have to face the entrance, but she still felt as if there were a spotlight shining right on her.

Petra pulled an electronic tablet device out of her leather bag, swiped her thumb across the screen, and started scrolling. Her eyes crinkled and she kept looking from Ivy to the tablet and back to Ivy again.

"Okay, seriously, what is going on?" Ivy demanded.

Petra's mouth was hanging open. The girls sitting at the tables nearest them leaned in closer. "How did you do it?" said Petra, shaking her head in slow motion. "It's amazing. How on *earth* did you do it?"

Before Ivy could ask her to explain, Petra handed Ivy the tablet. The Web browser was open to a concert review site featuring an article that covered the Pall Bearers' show in Franklin Grove.

SMALL TOWN, BIG SHOW: YESTERDAY'S PALL BEARERS CONCERT WAS TO DIE FOR

Oh my darkness! Ivy thumped her head with the heel of her hand. She had totally forgotten that she'd won VIP passes! She'd been looking forward to that concert for so long, and so had Sophia and Brendan. Ivy felt like she'd been staked. She hadn't been there, which meant that they hadn't gotten to go, either.

But wait—Ivy scanned farther down the page. From the review's photograph, it looked as if she *had* attended. Because there, holding a microphone, giving halfhearted devil's horns and doing her best to scream along, was her twin, Olivia—dressed up as Ivy herself.

Ivy read the caption: *The band brought superfan Ivy Vega onto the stage to perform their hit single "I Hate You."*

Ivy set the tablet down, not sure what to think.

"And this was yesterday?" asked Ivy.

Petra nodded. "Of course! Don't play coy."

But how . . . but why . . . ? It *must* have been Olivia, pretending to be her. Olivia at a Pall Bearers concert, though? She probably didn't know "I Hate You" from "Welcome to My Frightmare"! *Ugh!* She looked at the picture again. *Poor Olivia.* It *was* pretty funny.

She peered closer. There, with their elbows propped on the stage and hair flying as they rocked out, were Brendan and Sophia. This time Ivy laughed out loud. At least she didn't have to feel guilty about her friends missing the concert. Another win for Team Identical Twin!

Petra grabbed Ivy's arm, eyeing her intensely. "You have to tell me how you did it!"

"Did what?"

"Ivy!" Petra playfully slapped her. "*Hello*, you can drop the mysterious act for *me*, can't you? I'm your roommate! What's your secret?" She tapped the tablet. "How in Dracula's name did you pull this off?"

Understanding dawned on Ivy. The girls at Wallachia thought that Ivy had managed to go from Transylvania to Franklin Grove and back again—all in record time and without a single teacher spotting her! *Uh-oh. Time to set this straight.* She sucked in a deep breath.

"Look." She angled herself outward so that the eavesdroppers would be able to hear, too. Ivy was surrounded by a roomful of hopeful faces, watching her with wide eyes. They *wanted* her to have pulled this off, she realized as she looked around. Many of these girls had been students at Wallachia for years. In such a strict school, where there was an actual *obstacle course* separating boys and girls, how cool would it be if one of the students was so rebellious that she was able to get not just in and out of the Academy, but all the way to *America* and back without anybody noticing?

Who was Ivy to crush their dreams? She chose her words carefully. "I do love the Pall Bearers." She waited for the cheers, or even just an awed murmur, but instead there was dead silence. Worse, the smiles had dropped from their faces and they'd started to back away hastily. *Hang on!* thought Ivy. *Why are they suddenly treating me like I give off a bad smell?* Several of the girls had turned their backs and were now hunched over their meal trays. One girl glanced nervously over her shoulder and gave a small shriek before turning to whisper furiously in her friend's ear.

What the—?

Ivy heard the sound of heavy footsteps on the stone floor. A shudder ran up the length of her spine. A shadow fell over her. Ivy didn't have to turn around to know who was behind her. She craned her neck to look up and, sure enough, Avisrova was standing with her arms crossed and her face screwed up into an angry ball.

"I didn't expect my walk to lead me to this, Miss Lazar. You have some explaining to do."

Ivy's heart pounded in her chest. The newspaper with the photo of Ivy at a concert in

America was still on the screen in her hands.

Miss Avisrova had been waiting for something like this.

CHAPTER 6

Olivia kept working her jaw open and shut, trying to get her ears to pop. They hadn't stopped ringing since last night. And to top it off, her throat was raw from singing—well, more like *screaming*—up onstage with the Pall Bearers. Actually, she was sort of thankful for the sore throat. It meant she didn't have to say much to Brendan in the Meat & Greet. They had been here for thirty minutes and had probably said less than one word for each minute.

"So did you enjoy last night?" asked Brendan, looking a tad sheepish. *And so he should,* thought

Olivia. After all, he'd dragged her into it.

"If by 'enjoy' you mean 'endure,' then yes, it was okay."

Brendan looked out of the window, squirming in his seat. Olivia inspected her nails. She had never realized their friendship was so dependent on Ivy, but that was becoming *painfully* obvious. *Um, I could tell him about my bio-dad's wedding plans?* No, that would be a violation of her dad's trust. Her heart sank.

Brendan's knees bounced up and down under the booth. His attention was moving here, there, and everywhere. Olivia was pretty sure she'd caught him counting the ceiling tiles. When they left the concert last night, they should have been picking over every minute detail. Olivia knew that was what Ivy would have been doing with her boyfriend, if she'd been there. But that was just the problem—Brendan was Ivy's boyfriend, and he was only Olivia's friend because of that connection. Without Ivy there . . . Once Sophia had gone they'd waited for their ride home in near silence as all the other fans screamed and chatted around them. It couldn't have been more awkward—and now things were no better. They had to have something in common, didn't they?

We do, thought Olivia. *Ivy.* But too much talk about the one person they both missed would only bum them out—and this outing was supposed to be a fun distraction.

It had been Olivia's idea to hang out together at the Meat & Greet. She'd suggested it last night in the hope that they'd connect more when they weren't surrounded by screaming fans.

She took a sip of her fruit juice, looking out the window at the street. Hopefully she would see *something* that could spark a conversation.

"Hey, look at that bag!" Olivia cried, pointing to a girl in the street with a tote over her shoulder. "Leopard print is so up-to-the-minute. . . ." Her voice trailed off when she glanced back at Brendan. He was frowning at the bag as though it were an alien invader. Clearly, accessories weren't his thing. Brendan didn't care about this season's fashion, or any kind of fashion at all, for that matter. He had worn the same rock band T-shirts for as long as she'd known him. She sank farther into the booth.

There was a cute puppy being walked by a little girl with pigtails. *Would that work?* She snuck a glance at Brendan, but he was busy rubbing a thumb over his filed fangs. Olivia wrinkled her nose. Yeah, Brendan did not care about puppies— cute or not.

Olivia sighed. Parked alongside the curb was a flashy red Mustang with white racing stripes painted down the hood. *Cars* . . . Boys liked cars. *Ugh, but I don't know an engine from an exhaust pipe,* thought Olivia. Besides, she wasn't sure Brendan liked cars anyway. He was more of a music guru than a car buff. It was just too bad they didn't like any of the same bands!

A waitress in a grease-spattered white apron stopped by the table with an open notebook, pulling a pencil out from behind her ear. "Can I get you anything else?" she asked. Then a grin stretched across her lips, and she began pointing at Brendan and Olivia with the eraser on the end of her pencil. "Hey, are you two on a date? I could get you one milk shake with two straws!"

"No!" Olivia and Brendan burst out in unison. Olivia could feel her cheeks burning. This was so embarrassing, being mistaken for her sister's boyfriend's hot date. *I'd never do that to Ivy!*

"No, no, not at all," Brendan said, shaking his head emphatically. "You're totally wrong there." He gave Olivia a desperate glance, as though to say: *How did we get ourselves into this?* She gave him a smile back. This had seemed like such a good idea, and now it was all going wrong.

The waitress flipped her notepad shut. "Geez, just asking," she said, and scurried away without a backward glance.

Brendan sank back in his booth. "What was that about?" he asked, frowning in confusion.

"I don't know," Olivia said, folding her arms across her body. "She must be having a bad day or something. I think we probably need to find a way of getting out of here."

"Past her?" Brendan asked, chuckling and nodding to the waitress. She was telling off another customer for something. "Our glasses are still full—she'll never let us leave." He jerked a thumb at the glasses of juice. He was right. Olivia began to tap her fingers on her glass. Her fingers froze midtap. She had an idea. Looking out the window, she swished her hand across the table, knocking the glass off. "Oops!" she said, trying to sound surprised and staring at Brendan hard. "I'm such a klutz. . . ."

But Brendan had used his vampire reflexes and caught the fruit juice before it had even fallen from the table. Olivia's heart sank. *He didn't get it at all!* Ivy would have understood the escape plan right away.

Brendan offered a wry smile, setting the glass back on the table. Then he pointed out the window. "Look, Camilla's outside." Olivia turned. *How did I miss that?*

Olivia's best friend, Camilla, was squatting down in the bushes with a video camera and a French beret, filming one of her crazy scenes. Her lens was pointed at a boy in a snazzy pin-striped suit wearing full zombie makeup and lumbering down the sidewalk with his arms stretched out in front of him.

"Yeah! I guess I'd better go say hi. Do you want to come? That waitress can't *make* me finish my drink!" She slid out of the booth and waited.

"No, you go ahead." He smiled at Olivia as if

to say: *It's probably best if we leave it here.* She knew he wasn't being mean; it was just that there was a big Ivy-shaped space between them.

"See you later, then," Olivia said, and walked quickly past the waitress, who was scowling at a receipt.

At the door of the Meat & Greet, Olivia looked back to see Brendan breathing a big sigh of relief and resting his head back on the cushioned booth behind him. Any other day she would have been offended, but today, she knew how he felt.

Outside, Olivia hurried down the street, but she couldn't see Camilla. Where did she go? There was another girl from Franklin Grove Middle School, though—Aurora. She was leaning against a wall doing absolutely nothing, wearing a fabulous sequined gown more fit for prom or the Oscars than a normal weekday afternoon. *Now, that's style,* thought Olivia, marching over to her.

"Hey, Aurora! I totally love your outfit. Did you see where Camilla—?"

"Cut!"

Olivia jumped as Camilla popped out from

behind a mailbox across the street, holding her camera.

"Olivia! You ruined the take!" Camilla crossed the street wearing black skinny jeans, ballet flats, and a scarf tied around her neck. Ever since she had written and directed the school play, *Romezog and Julietron*, she had become quite the passionate filmmaker. She'd even been on a trip to film in Paris.

"I'm so sorry!" Olivia clasped her hand over her mouth. "I didn't see you there. I mean, I saw you before, and I wanted to know where you were, and . . ." She was gesturing wildly trying to explain herself. "I wandered into your scene, didn't I? I'm so sorry." Olivia had prided herself on her filmmaking expertise ever since starring in a film with Jackson. How could she have been such a fool?

"It's okay." Camilla smiled, picking up her black-and-white clipboard. She erased "Take Two" and wrote "Take Three." "I'm experimenting with a new documentary, hidden-camera style, blending it with the classical forties film noir look." Olivia had no idea what that meant, but she nodded along.

"That's why I'm all dressed up with nowhere to go," grumbled Aurora, picking up the train of her gown.

Camilla placed her hands on her hips. "Do you want to be introduced to Craig Cash or not?"

Olivia almost gasped. Aurora and Craig Cash? Tall, popular, athletic—Craig was one of the most eligible guys in the whole school.

"Oh, wow, that's amazing!" Olivia started to say. She'd love to find out all about this. But Camilla was frowning at her. *Um, I know when I'm not wanted,* Olivia thought. *I can take a hint!*

"Maybe I'll see you later, then?" she told Camilla. She didn't want to throw off their movie any more.

Camilla was already busy repositioning Aurora so that she looked more "old Hollywood" by leaning up against the wall. She waved a hand over her shoulder without even looking around.

"Later."

"Maybe we could get pizza tonight?" Olivia called. She waited for a response but none came. She slunk away, starting down Orange Grove Avenue and heading back to her house. She couldn't ignore the pain of—was it loneliness?—in her chest. For the first time since Ivy had gone to Wallachia Academy, Olivia had to admit the truth to herself. *Who am I kidding? I've been miserable since the moment she left.* Olivia almost never walked home from town on her own; Ivy was usually there to tease her about the latest pink outfit she'd bought or complain about the newest rom com film she'd been persuaded to sit through.

She remembered her mom dropping her off on her first day at Franklin Grove. She had been intimidated by the campus, which had looked ancient in comparison to her former school's ugly modern building. Franklin Grove had leafy vines, huge columns, and a yawning hallway. Olivia recalled staring up at it and being terrified that she would be the friendless new girl forever. But all that had changed quickly, and Olivia had even been put in charge of the biggest social event at school.

That was almost a year ago. Now, in the space of just a few minutes, she had felt like both Brendan and Camilla were strangers. Plus, of course, her sister was on the other side of the Atlantic. Olivia was beginning to feel like an outsider all over again. She knew this was probably part of growing up—that one day she and Ivy would be leading their own lives—but why did it have to be so horrible right now? *I'm not ready for this!* She didn't even have a boyfriend to call anymore.

Olivia scuffed her wedges along the sidewalk, sticking her hands in the pockets of her pink bubble skirt. On a day like today, dressing like Ivy would have fitted her mood much better!

Loitering outside the grocery store were Garrick Stevens and his buddies, nicknamed the Beasts by everyone in Franklin Grove. Garrick was bouncing a basketball loudly on the pavement when he looked up, noticing Olivia.

"Watch out!" He faked throwing the ball at her. Olivia didn't flinch. They could try their scary act on her all they wanted, but Olivia wasn't afraid of the Beasts anymore. She had seen all they could do and, frankly, it wasn't much.

"Think you're tough?" said Garrick. He and his Beastly buddies formed a circle around her, forcing her to stop. She was surrounded by evil snickers and sneers. Their breath was so bad it should have come with big yellow and black warning signs: DANGER! BIOHAZARD!

Olivia wrinkled her nose and tried to leave, but Garrick blocked her. "Where's your little bunny boyfriend, *Olivia*?" He frowned and pretended to rub tears from his eyes with his fists. "Oh, that's right. Didn't he break up with you? Boohoo."

"Very funny," said Olivia through gritted teeth. A cosmic black hole was opening up in the bottom of her stomach.

Garrick put on a fake baby voice. "Oooh, is Ivy not here to protect you anymore?"

Olivia rolled her eyes. "Excuse me," she said, once again trying to get out of the circle.

"I don't think so." Garrick leered at her. "Because I don't see Ivy anywhere." He pretended to look around.

"Listen, buddy." Olivia poked Garrick in the chest. "You must be a *real* coward if you are that scared of one little girl!" *Whoa, where did that come from?*

Garrick's face darkened. "I'll bite you for that."

The boys tightened the circle around her. Garrick bared his teeth. Suddenly, Olivia felt suffocated.

"Get away from me, or I'll—I'll . . ."

"You'll what?" interrupted Garrick. "You don't have your sister now. You don't even have your Hollywood boyfriend. Like you were ever going to keep *him*!" Garrick brought his face close to hers. "A-list stars don't date nobodies. And without him and Ivy, that's what you are—a nobody."

Olivia could feel her face crumpling. Then . . . *Ding, ding! Ding, ding!* Was that a bicycle bell? A figure appeared from around the corner, riding a blue vintage-style bicycle. The girl leaned low over her handlebars, aiming straight for the Beasts. They leaped out of the way as she slammed on her brakes and sent the back wheel skidding out so that the boys' legs were nearly knocked out from under them. They scattered just in time, yelping in protest. One of them fell on the ground, limbs flailing. The others bent to help him up, dusting him off. Looking at them over the handlebars of the bike was Holly.

"Are you crazy?" yelled Garrick.

Holly was wearing a long, flower-power summer dress, and a camera dangled from around her neck. Her hair was dyed with gorgeous bright red streaks.

"You could have hurt someone," said another Beast as Holly came to a stop next to Olivia.

Olivia furrowed her eyebrows and got up in Garrick's face. "You guys are so tough until somebody stands up to you. Isn't that right?"

He stepped back, rubbing the back of his neck. "Whatever," he mumbled.

Holly tapped her camera. "You guys better leave or I'll take a few more pictures of you harassing an innocent girl. How would you like that?"

Garrick's eyes went wide, and he held up his hands in surrender. "Okay, okay. We're going!"

Olivia knew that Garrick wouldn't want the authorities looking at those pictures. That might lead to people snooping around, and if the vampire community wanted to maintain their secrecy, they couldn't afford any prying. The Beasts were dumb, but they weren't *that* dumb. She could feel her whole body trembling as they backed away, and she loosened the silk scarf at her throat. *Thank goodness Holly turned up when she did.* Olivia hated to admit it, but she hadn't been sure how she was going to hold it together just then.

Garrick grabbed his basketball and motioned for the other Beasts to follow, throwing a final filthy look in Olivia's direction. They wandered off, grumbling and playfully shoving one another.

"That's it," called Holly after them. "Go home and take a shower!" She turned to Olivia, cupping Olivia's elbow. "Are you okay?"

"Yeah." She smoothed her skirt. "It's not the first time I've had a run-in with those guys." But the mention of Jackson had shaken her in a way that none of the other close calls had. Olivia hugged her arms to her chest. The Beasts had actually been right about one thing—she didn't have Jackson and she didn't have Ivy. For the first time ever, Olivia Abbott was lonely.

Holly stared after Garrick and company as they walked down the street. "Does this sort of thing happen a lot in Franklin Grove?" She dismounted her bike.

"It's almost like an occupational hazard," said Olivia, again remembering her first day at school, when Ivy had saved her from being picked on by the Beasts.

"Come here and take a breather," Holly told

Olivia, leading her to a bus stop bench. They sat down together, and Holly positioned her camera on her lap. She clicked the "on" button and the viewfinder lit up. "Want to see some of my photos?" she asked.

"Sure." Olivia nodded. Her voice sounded smaller than usual.

Holly began scrolling through the pictures stored on her camera. The first one was of a brightly painted sign that read: FRANKLIN GROVE ANIMAL RESCUE.

"Hey, those aren't the Beasts!" Olivia pointed at the pictures of tail-wagging dogs. Holly giggled at a pug with drool hanging out of both sides of his mouth and a goofy, lopsided dog grin.

"Are you sure?" Holly asked. "Because I think this one could definitely be mistaken for Garrick!"

Olivia doubled over laughing until she got a stitch and had to clutch her sides. "Thank goodness you were around to put those boys in their place," she said, wiping her eyes. Olivia had thought she was headed for a meltdown, but Holly had managed to cheer her up in no time. Maybe she wasn't as totally alone as she'd thought. . . .

Holly frowned. "Well, don't worry. I'll always back you up."

Olivia gave Holly a hug. After feeling so abandoned today, it was nice that someone was around to support her. *I think I'm going to be seeing a lot more of this girl in the future,* thought Olivia happily.

"So, how about we make good on that rain check?" asked Holly. Olivia cocked her head, confused. "I mean, do you want to come over to my house?"

"Oh, yeah!" Olivia jumped up. "Definitely."

"Far out!" Holly exclaimed. Her unique style, Olivia figured, was going to take a little getting used to.

They walked together, Holly alongside her bicycle, holding on to the handlebars.

"Do you want to give your sister a call so that she can come along, too?" asked Holly. "I'd really like to meet her." Olivia was about to remind her that Ivy was out of the country when Holly continued. "It's not like I have any music that she'd like to listen to, but we can still hang out. I mean, the Pall Bearers take some getting used to, right?"

That was when Olivia understood—the pictures of her at the concert! Holly thought that had been Ivy, back from Transylvania.

"Holly, those are just—" Olivia started to explain when Holly's phone beeped. She held up one finger, checking the incoming text.

"So sorry, Olivia, but I've really got to run." She waved her phone. "But we'll talk later, okay? I can't wait to meet Ivy and ask her all about Transylvania. Maybe get some cool pictures of her, too." Holly was talking fast. "If I could get the lowdown on Europe from her, I know it would really help me break through as a journalist. There's a travel writing competition with a deadline at the end of the week—writers need to interview someone who's explored the world. And Ivy would be so cool in photos, too, if she's just like you say she is!"

"Um, yeah," Olivia muttered. "She's totally cool. And thanks for everything—I really appreciate what you did back there." But Holly wasn't listening. She'd already hopped back on her bike and was pedaling furiously in the opposite direction.

How could Olivia thank Holly properly? She couldn't bear the thought of telling her Ivy wasn't around to have a photo taken of her. *But if she doesn't get her interview, her dreams of breaking into journalism will be over before she's written a word. I'd feel terrible!* An idea started to form. A dangerously clever idea . . .

Olivia had dressed as Ivy to wrangle tickets to a concert. Surely she could do the same to help her new friend's career? If there was one thing Olivia was short on right now, it was friends. And Holly had really been there for her when she needed someone. In Olivia's book, that counted for a lot.

She remembered what it had been like at the start of her acting career. Auditioning for *The Groves* had been terrifying. It would be fine to help Holly get the pictures she needed—Olivia could dress up like Ivy one last time.

It was the right thing to do.

Wasn't it?

CHAPTER 7

Ivy woke with a start. She'd heard something—
and there it was again—the creak of a coffin lid
opening. She squeezed the side of her digital
watch and the screen lit up. Midnight. Ivy peered
out of her coffin to see Petra slipping out of hers,
quietly closing the lid so as not to wake the other
girls. Ivy watched as Petra shoved her feet into a
pair of sneakers sitting near the door and crept
out of the room.

Ivy lay back down on the cool, velvet lining
of her coffin, staring into the darkness. *Petra's
going to see Etan. I just know it.* Love made

people do crazy things. Ivy's eyelids were heavy. She'd had only a few hours of sleep and she wanted to let Petra go. She'd already been in a ton of trouble after Miss Avisrova had seen the article about "Ivy" being at the Pall Bearers concert. She'd been made to clean out the cages for every bat in the school! *I'm not getting myself into any more scrapes for anyone,* Ivy thought now. *No way.*

But could she stay in this warm coffin and let Petra make a bad decision? *What would Olivia do?* She opened her eyes and gave a loud sigh. Of course, it was obvious what Olivia would do— she'd go and help Petra. *Why me? Why do I have to feel guilty about letting Petra go out into the dark on her own?* Ivy rubbed her eyes. She couldn't let Petra get into trouble, and trouble was exactly what Petra was going to find if she tried to cross the Gauntlet to see her crush.

Ivy opened her coffin, crawled out, and shut the lid, pushing the middle of the Wallachia crest emblazoned on the top to lock it. She slid into her black tennis shoes and threw her coat on over her T-shirt and sweatpants. Soft snoring could be heard coming from the other coffins in Ivy's dorm room. Her roommates were fast asleep. *Petra had better appreciate this,* she thought as she tiptoed out the door.

In the chilly corridor, Ivy thought she heard a rustling noise behind her, but when she whipped around, no one was there. That was strange. Her vampire hearing usually never failed her.

She continued down the hallway, slipped back the bolt on a large ornate door, and gently closed it behind her.

Outside, Ivy hugged herself, rubbing her arms. At night, the grounds of Wallachia Academy were the most eerie thing she had ever seen. The whole place looked like a graveyard on Halloween. The stone facade of the school building glowed ghostly pale in the moonlight. The trimmed hedges looked alive in the night breeze. Every creak of a branch and crunch of leaves sounded threatening.

Ivy tried to tune her hearing to focus on Petra. She could hear Petra's sneakers sinking into the soft grass and soil. She picked up her pace. Yep—

judging from the direction of her footsteps, Petra was definitely headed for the spooky, booby-trapped forest that divided the girls' and boys' dorms.

Ivy hurried over, not caring whether she was heard or not. She found Petra at the edge of the wood, staring at a narrow passageway that began between two birch trees.

"Are you nuts?" Ivy hissed.

"No, I'm in love." Petra clasped her hands together. "My whole heart aches. Do you know what that feels like?"

"Of course I know what that feels like. My own boyfriend is all the way back in America, which, let me remind you, is much farther away than the other side of a forest."

Petra flapped her hand, batting aside Ivy's comment. She was holding an envelope, which Ivy was sure contained another drawing or sappy poem. "If you really loved him, you would never have left."

"What?!" Ivy didn't know whether to laugh or scream—*vampires and their ridiculous ideas of romance!* Ivy took a deep breath. "This isn't going to solve anything," she told Petra. "You're only going to get caught in one of the booby traps, and a teacher is going to have to rescue you, and you'll be in an epic amount of trouble. What would that accomplish?"

Petra pressed the back of her hand to her forehead in true dramatic fashion. "You don't understand. I have to prove myself to Etan!" She charged into the woods.

"Wait!" Ivy barreled in after her.

The forest was pitch-black. Even with vampire sight, Ivy could barely see through it. She could only just make out the dim figure of Petra running ahead. They hadn't gotten more than ten feet when Petra tripped over a hidden wire. She stumbled forward, landing in the dirt. The wire triggered a wasps' nest, which swung down from a tree on a rope. Ivy grabbed Petra and dragged her off to the side just as the nest smashed into another tree trunk. Buzzing filled the air. But before they could run, the ground gave way beneath them. Ivy scrambled back, pulling Petra with her.

The forest floor opened up into a pit. Ivy peered over the edge. There were no spikes, like in medieval movies; instead foul-smelling black goo gurgled inside.

Petra was swatting at the wasps flying overhead.

"Be careful!" Ivy flung one arm over her head, using the other to push Petra to safety a few paces down the path. "Well, this has been fun," she said, coming to a stop. "But let's go back now."

Petra brandished the envelope, now crumpled and dirty from their narrow escapes. "Absolutely not. I have to get this to Etan! You can go back. You don't have to come with me." She turned and continued down the path.

Ivy huffed. This girl was getting on her last nerve! But even though Ivy wanted to strangle her, she couldn't let Petra bumble through this deadly obstacle course alone. She trotted after her friend, careful to watch where she stepped. Petra was taking boy-crazy to a brand-new level. Ivy wondered if she would do the same for Brendan. *Probably . . . but I definitely wouldn't admit that to him!*

She caught up with Petra, who looked at her in surprise, then smiled.

"Okay, I'll admit it," she said. "I'm glad you're here."

They started up a gradual incline. The tree limbs groaned in the wind, and Ivy held Petra's hand to keep her from freaking out. Suddenly, there was a sharp twang, and Ivy shoved Petra sideways, out of the path. She was just about to dive out of the way herself when a snapping rope coiled around her ankles, lifting her feet out from under her and dragging her high up into the trees. The blood rushed to her head. She'd been caught!

"Help me," she whispered, but Petra was frozen.

Ivy listened. A bat darted through the air, skimming past their noses. Then slow, confident footsteps crunched toward them. She knew who it was even before she heard the voice speak.

"Well, well," said Miss Avisrova as she approached Petra.

"S-s-sorry," said Petra, bowing her head. "I—I—I don't know what I was thinking."

Ivy stared down at the severe parting in Miss Avisrova's hair. Their teacher curled her fingers around the back of Petra's neck. "You will come with me back to the girls' dormitory immediately." She started to guide Petra down the path.

Petra looked upward. "Miss, there's someone else up—"

Avisrova cut her off and repeated herself, more forcefully this time. "You *will* accompany me back to the girls' dormitory. Immediately."

"But—"

"But nothing," Avisrova snapped. "I don't know what you are talking about. Honestly. A girl on her own in the Gauntlet at night . . . No student from the Academy could possibly escape the Gauntlet."

Petra's mouth worked, but no words came out. Ivy couldn't believe it. Avisrova had to know that someone else was in the forest. She was a vampire, with vampire senses, and she had caught Petra red-handed. No, Miss Avisrova was *choosing* to let Ivy dangle alone in the Gauntlet.

Petra glanced back anxiously at Ivy as she was led away. She shrugged, and Ivy's chest heaved with fury. Her eyes narrowed. Ivy knew Avisrova wanted her to call for help, but too bad. That evil teacher was going to be sorely disappointed, because no way was Ivy Vega giving her that satisfaction.

No student can escape the Gauntlet, huh? Ivy's blood boiled. Was that what Avisrova thought? Well, apparently, Miss Avisrova did not know the first thing about Ivy.

As soon as her teacher was out of sight and earshot, Ivy began swinging back and forth like a pendulum. Her muscles strained and the cord around her ankles cut into her skin. It took a few minutes, but finally she got enough momentum and swung herself up to grab hold of the rope.

Take this, Avisrova. Ivy's arms trembled as she held herself right side up. She ripped into the rope with her teeth, gnawing at the threads with her newly grown fangs until she heard a *snap*. Moments later, she landed on the ground with a loud *thump*.

She lay on her back, waiting for agonizing pain to shoot up one of her limbs, but . . . nothing. Tentatively, she felt the ground beneath her and lifted up a fistful of soft brown leaves. She sat up and looked around her. *How lucky am I?* Ivy had landed in a pile of foliage that had broken her fall.

The leaves were gathered in a neat circle, almost as though someone had arranged them there.

Out of the corner of her eye, Ivy noticed Petra's envelope. It was half-covered in dirt. She picked it up and dusted it off. Whatever it was, Petra must have worked pretty hard on it to go to this much trouble just to make a delivery. That meant she would definitely want it back.

Ivy checked to make sure nothing had fallen out of her own pockets while she'd been dangling by her feet. She was about to follow Petra and Avisrova out of the woods when she paused and looked back over her shoulder. She could only imagine the hidden grass snakes, the hairy spiders, and, of course, the trip wires that lay in the forest beyond. She remembered the story about the girl whose hair turned white because of the Gauntlet. What had she seen? But another thought wormed its way up Ivy's brain. . . . *Could I complete the obstacle course?* That would prove a point to Avisrova and to the entire school. Ivy shouldn't let silly ghost stories scare her! If one person was able to emerge on the other side of the Gauntlet, Wallachia Academy might drag itself into the twenty-first century. *Maybe.*

"I mean, the whole Gauntlet thing is ridiculous," Ivy said out loud, trying to talk herself into being brave. "I need to show this school how stuffy and old-fashioned things like this are—and prove that it doesn't even work!" If Ivy could get across . . . perhaps the school would give up on keeping the boys and girls apart, and Petra might even get to talk to—instead of just stare at—her beloved Etan.

Ivy knew the plan was reckless, but wasn't that what Ivy was known for at Wallachia? That was it—her mind was made up. The only real question left was how to conquer the Gauntlet successfully. She thought back to Helga's advice in the classroom. What was it she'd said? "Knowledge and strength are a person's most important assets." Ivy had some knowledge of plants, and she could dig deep for the strength she needed. *I can do this!* But what first? *Okay, how to avoid those booby-trap trip wires on the ground . . . ?*

Ivy walked over to one of the largest trees in the forest. Without hesitating, she reached for the lowest branch and pulled herself up until she was straddling it. She climbed higher, using the sturdier limbs as a makeshift ladder. Luckily, the forest was dense and the trees so close together that she could move from one to the next, making her way through the forest without touching the ground. She grabbed ahold of a long branch from one of the trees nearby. She carefully swung herself to the neighboring trunk, as if she were a pirate boarding an enemy ship.

Ivy hopped and jumped from one tree to another, panting with the exertion. This was worse than Physical Education back in Franklin Grove! But after a while, she reached the edge of the woods, just as the sun was beginning to peek out over the horizon. Ivy watched as oranges, pinks, and yellows spilled out over the clouds. She had to admit: Transylvania did have one of the most beautiful landscapes in the world.

The morning glow curled around the trunks, illuminating several patches of the Oxynamon plant Helga had shown them in class. Ivy had never seen it grow like this in the human world, like it was growing out of the tree and wrapping itself around the bark. She tore off two bunches.

If anyone saw her, she could say she had been doing some extra-credit work for Herbal Science. She stuffed it in her pocket, took out Petra's envelope, and jumped down from the last tree.

I did it! She had to stop herself from squealing. That would definitely not suit the cool-girl Ivy persona she was trying to build. But here she was on the other side of the Gauntlet, standing in the shadow of the boys' dormitory. Stone walls, high-rising turrets . . . It looked just the same as the girls' dorms to Ivy. *What's the big deal, exactly?* She leaned her head to the side, to view it at another angle. Transylvanian vampires and their ideas of romance—it would never make sense to her.

A handsome face appeared in one of the frosted windows of the boys' dormitory. Ivy squinted to try to make it out. The boy held up one finger and then disappeared.

Seconds later, he came rushing out onto the dew-stained lawn. Ivy didn't know which was more amusing: his bedhead or his look of sheer amazement.

"Where's Petra?" he cried, stumbling to a halt. "What are you doing here?" He looked past Ivy hopefully, scanning the forest, before his gaze settled back on her face. He cleared his throat. "Um, there seems to be a misunderstanding. You're very nice and everything, but Petra's my true love. I mean, I'm sure some boys would find you attractive, but—"

"Don't kid yourself!" Ivy erupted. She couldn't believe it. Etan thought she'd made her way through the Gauntlet because—because . . . *He thinks I have a crush on him!* Ivy pulled her shoulders back. "I have the best boyfriend in the world waiting for me back in Franklin Grove. I'm not here because I 'heart' you!" She drew a little heart in the air with her forefingers, grimacing. "I'm here to help Petra."

Before Etan could open his mouth to apologize, there was the sound of a twig snapping. He jumped and darted back inside. Ivy looked around.

That was weird. Why was everyone around here so jumpy? *Thank goodness I have a normal boyfriend. Just not here in Transylvania.* Ivy sighed. Maybe she had made the wrong—

A slow clap started up behind her. "Bravo, bravo."

Bats alive! Ivy's heart jolted. She turned to see Miss Avisrova, wearing an ugly frown. How did her teacher get here so fast?

Ivy's jaw clenched. *Here it comes.*

"You know"—the Etiquette teacher circled her—"I smelled you, Miss Lazar, there in the forest, from a mile away. And I knew that you would have the insolence to try to complete the course."

"I *did* complete the course," Ivy corrected.

Miss Avisrova ignored her. "That ostentatious American fragrance creates an unmistakable stench."

It's got to smell better than Eau de Snob, thought Ivy, but she just managed to bite her lip. *Do not say that out loud.* There was no way that would end well.

Miss Avisrova snatched the grubby envelope from Ivy's hand. "What do we have here?" She read the scrawling script. "Very well," she said sharply. "As is customary, the token of love will be passed on to the intended."

Ivy frowned. On the one hand, she was glad that Petra's letter would get to her true love. But on the other hand . . . "What do you mean by

126

'customary'?" she asked. Had the Gauntlet been conquered by love before?

Avisrova's eyebrows nearly disappeared into her hairline. "I don't have to explain my meaning to you," she said, her voice high and tight. Then she seemed to force herself to relax, her shoulders dropping. "But even I have a heart. Etan will get his letter." For a moment, Avisrova gazed off in the direction of the boys' dormitory. "I was in love once, you know. . . ." *In love?* Ivy could *not* picture that. But as fast as this softer side had come on, Avisrova's stony expression returned. She cleared her throat. "As for you, Miss Lazar . . ." The hairs on the back of Ivy's neck stood on end. "You will report to my office this afternoon." She glanced over toward the Gauntlet, a smile twitching at the corners of her mouth. "But you'd better be quick. I want you back in your dorm room before anyone wakes up."

How completely fantastic, thought Ivy, squinting into the rising sun as Avisrova walked off in the direction of the boys' dorm. *Now I have to get back through the forest without my hair turning white and then wait for my death sentence.* She tried not to shiver in the chill dawn air, and wondered what her sister was doing right now. *Olivia would never get herself into trouble like this,* she thought. Why couldn't Ivy be more like her twin?

CHAPTER 8

Low: 90
High: 96
Current Temperature: 92

Olivia snapped shut the pink rhinestone cover on her phone. Of course the universe wouldn't cooperate just so that she could pull off a lie. The best she could hope for now was to get out of her house without being spotted by anyone—especially her parents.

She clicked on her webcam, and Ivy appeared at her desk on-screen. She and Ivy had been texting and Ivy had agreed to take a quick ten minutes during her lunch break to have a video chat with Olivia.

"Hey there, sister!" Olivia waved to the camera. "How do I look?"

Ivy's eyes got wide. "Awful! What are you wearing?"

Olivia looked at the corner of the screen that showed her own picture as Ivy would see it through her computer. She had lined her eyes with dark eyeliner and coated her lips with a thick layer of Midnight Mauve lipstick. Her dark hair was pinned into a bun with two chopsticks.

Olivia shrugged. "You know what they say—'Imitation is the sincerest form of flattery.' And anyway, you look a bit—um—rough around the edges yourself." She didn't want to say too much, but her sister looked as though she'd been dragged through a hedge backward!

Ivy hastily patted down her hair. "I had a bit of a midnight adventure," she said.

"Oh, nice!" Olivia cried, clapping her hands together. "A midnight feast? I knew you'd make friends quickly. Tell me all about it!"

Olivia saw Ivy stifle a yawn on-screen. "It wasn't a feast, exactly, more of an assault course." Olivia felt her face crease in a frown, but Ivy carried on talking. "I'll tell you about it some other time. Once I've had a good night's sleep. You fill me in on what you've been doing. What's with the Goth makeup?"

"Um, see, I may have gotten myself caught up in a teensy little lie." Olivia held her fingers an inch apart. "The thing is, well, I made this new friend named Holly and she really wanted to meet you and interview you about Transylvania. She's training to be a journalist and has entered a travel writing competition and . . . she thinks you're back in the country."

Ivy palmed her forehead.

"What? I couldn't exactly tell her you were at a vampire boarding school! Plus, she thinks getting pictures of you will help her win the competition, and I don't want to let her down. The deadline is the end of this week."

Ivy shook her head, clucking her tongue. "Olivia, Olivia, Olivia." She broke out into a mischievous grin. "Don't forget to bring your best death stare. At least I know you can fool people that you're me, what with the Pall Bearers concert and everything!"

"You heard about that!" Olivia hid her face behind her hands as her shoulders shook with laughter.

"Yes, we heard about it! And I got into a whole lot of trouble. My teacher thought I'd skipped school to go to a concert."

Olivia's hands fell from her face. "I'm so sorry!" She couldn't believe it. *I got my twin into trouble by trying to help her boyfriend!*

Ivy batted a hand through the air. "Forget about it. I seem to get in trouble a lot here." Her smile faded.

"You're not still feeling homesick, are you?" Olivia asked, suddenly concerned.

Ivy shrugged. "Kind of. A little. What about you? How are you feeling now that you're single again? Everything okay?"

Olivia smiled bravely. "Getting better. One day at a time."

A bell rang out from Ivy's end. "Oops, that must be the end of our lunch hour. Talk later, sis!" Ivy giggled and signed off.

Olivia's palms were getting sweaty now and her heart was thumping in her chest. What if she messed this up?

She tiptoed down the stairs from her bedroom, straightening her black wig. How would she explain the long coat and hooded jacket she was wearing? It was going to be a scorcher in Franklin Grove today, and this outfit certainly didn't fit in with Olivia's usual fashion sense. This was the same outfit she'd worn to the Pall Bearers concert.

What am I doing? What am I thinking? Olivia was starting to freak out. *Do I really think I can pull this off?* Once could have been a fluke. Twice? That might be asking for too much luck. And how did she wind up having to cover one lie with another lie? *I* had *to tell the first lie,* Olivia told herself for the thirtieth time that morning. She hadn't had a choice. It was either that or disappoint Brendan and Sophia.

Still, somehow she had a feeling that this was not going to end well.

One last step and . . . *Creaaaaaaaaak!* Olivia cringed.

"Olivia, are you there?" her adoptive mother, Mrs. Abbott, called. *Oh no!* She made a beeline for the front door, but her mom stepped out of the living room just as she was reaching for the handle. "Why are you wearing that big coat, dear?"

Olivia reached for her hood, dragging it off quickly, along with the black Ivy wig. Now, as far as Mrs. Abbott knew, her daughter was just in a hoodie and not dressed in a full-on Ivy disguise. Olivia dug a pair of sunglasses out of the pocket of her coat and shoved them over her nose. *Think, Olivia.* "Oh, um . . ." She squeezed her eyes shut for a split second, and when she turned around she had shaped her lips into her trademark mega-watt smile. "I'm going over to Charles's later, you know." She tried to sound offhand. "To talk wedding stuff. The plans are still all very hush-hush, remember, and I figure I'll be coming back with notepads and bridal magazines and vacation brochures. So, I needed something with big pockets." She opened them up to demonstrate. When Olivia had been acting in her first film, *The Groves*, the mega-famous Hollywood studio head,

Harker, had told her, "Hey, kid, the key to selling any role is first confidence and then the details."

Mrs. Abbott shrugged, looking a bit befuddled. "Okay, that's fine. Have fun, and I hope you don't get too hot in that thing."

Olivia shut the door behind her, replacing the wig and hood so that she was re-Ivy-ed. *I swear, if I get through this little mess I've made, I will never tell another lie ever again.*

★ 🐰 ★

Olivia checked her reflection in the window of Mister Smoothie. She looked like Ivy, but with a tan. She slipped off the coat and draped it over her arm. Holly didn't know why Ivy was always so pale, so Olivia should be able to get away with it. Ivy could have been outside a lot while on vacation in Europe. Olivia almost burst out laughing at the thought. Ivy Vega volunteering for outdoor activities? The thought was ridiculous.

Olivia glanced at her watch and started going over the plan one more time in her head. It was ten a.m. She would go inside, pretending to be Ivy. She would tell Holly that Olivia wouldn't be long, but that they should begin without her. That would give Holly a chance to take some photos. At 10:22, Sophia would call Olivia's phone. Ivy/Olivia would act as if the real Olivia was on the phone. Then Ivy/Olivia would tell Holly that Olivia was stuck at their father's house helping him with something and that Ivy was needed there right away, too. The three of them would have to hang out together some other time. *Like when Ivy gets back from Transylvania,* thought Olivia.

Simple, right?

Olivia took a deep breath. It would be a miracle if she made it through the day without having a heart attack! The door chimed as she stepped inside Mister Smoothie. She did a quick scan of the restaurant, spotting Holly right away with her long red streaks of hair. She was sitting in a corner booth with her back to the door.

Olivia started to walk over. *Hold on. . . .* Ivy wouldn't know who Holly was, or what she looked like. The two had never met. She wouldn't just walk over there, would she? "No," Olivia muttered under her breath. "Play it cool." That was what Ivy would do, and Olivia needed to sell the part. *It's all in the details,* she reminded herself.

Okay, where to go first? Olivia headed for the opposite side of Mister Smoothie. That should throw Holly off the trail. She strolled around, making sure to look at all the customers.

A girl in a football jersey and jeans looked up from stirring her Mocha Choca Latte smoothie. "What are you looking at, Goth Girl?"

Olivia froze in place. If she were the real Ivy, she'd have something witty to say. *Not at you, Smoothie Drinker.* No, that was terrible. *Try kicking a football someplace else, Jersey Girl.* That was even lamer. Nothing else was coming to mind, so Olivia just made an awkward shrug and moved on to another booth.

When she'd pretend-inspected nearly all the available booths, Olivia decided she had kept the charade up long enough. Walking over to where Holly was sitting and fiddling with her camera, Olivia tapped her on the shoulder. "Are you Olivia's pal?" *Pal? Who says* pal *anymore?*

Holly put down her camera and looked "Ivy" over. She smiled. "Yes." She extended a hand. "I'm Holly. It's great to finally meet you. How was Transylvania?"

Olivia scooted into the pink leather booth opposite Holly. "It was good. Actually, I'm headed back tomorrow." She had rehearsed the cover story. If Ivy had to go back across the Atlantic, there was no way Holly could expect another get-together. Olivia couldn't handle pulling this switcheroo every single day! "Yeah, it sucks," she finished.

Holly frowned. "Didn't you just say it was good?"

Olivia suppressed her instinct to laugh nervously. That was *so* not Ivy. But what a fool she was! Bunnies didn't know that *sucks* meant *good* in vampire speak. And she couldn't explain that to Holly without outing all of vampire society.

I'll just have to improvise. She put one elbow on the table and picked at the Midnight Mauve polish she'd painted on her nails. "Oh, you know, I don't like to play by the rules. I'd rather give words my own meanings. 'Sucks' means 'totally cool.' In Ivy-speak, I mean."

"I like it," said Holly enthusiastically. "In fact," she continued, turning on her camera, "I'm really digging your whole vibe. That look"—she shaped her fingers into a rectangular frame—"the hair, the makeup, the rocker T-shirt and jeans . . . It's so . . . open-minded. I can tell you're a traveler of the world. Do you mind if I take a few pictures?"

"Snap away." Olivia set her phone down on the table and tried to pull off her best tough-girl poses. Some of the other customers were staring at her oddly, and she tried not to feel self-conscious or worry that they recognized her. *Be brave!* she told herself, folding her arms over her chest. She tried flexing her biceps for the camera. *How completely embarrassing,* she thought, once again thankful that Ivy wasn't here to witness her horrible impersonation.

"Another look," Holly directed. "Pretend you're gazing out over an African desert."

Olivia gazed into the distance, brooding . . . and nearly jumped out of her skin. There was Brendan, outside the window, staring at her openmouthed. Olivia gulped and quickly glanced away. *This will be okay,* she tried to tell herself.

At least Holly didn't seem to suspect anything. She kneeled on the tiled floor of Mister

Smoothie, catching various angles. Olivia listened to the *click, click, click,* but she could see Brendan walking over, waving excitedly. Her mouth felt dry and it was all she could do to maintain her cool composure.

Holly lowered her camera just as Brendan burst through the doors. "That's a wrap!" she said, beaming. "I can't tell you how much this means to me. Olivia said so many great things about you—I couldn't wait to meet you and get a few photos. I really want to launch my career one day, and interesting subjects will make all the difference." Her eyes twinkled. Brendan was getting nearer, his arms wide in anticipation of a hug. "Getting an exclusive with you is a real privilege," Holly carried on. "You don't know how much this could help me win the travel writing competition."

"That's killer." Olivia could hardly get the words out. Brendan was making his way between the booths, his eyes fixed on Olivia's face. She had to stop this! She sent Brendan a sharp shake of her head and he paused, realizing something was wrong.

"Do you want a smoothie?" she asked Holly,

taking her arm and steering her around so that her back was to Brendan. "My treat."

"Sure, thanks!" Holly read the menu, picking from the list of crazy-named fruit drinks. "Can you get me a Twist and Shout?"

Olivia tried not to groan. Would it be completely awful of her to tell one more white lie—that Mister Smoothie was out of Twist and Shouts? She wasn't sure she could bear hearing that song again—not when she was already so on edge. Just thinking about it made her shiver:

> *Well, shake up your smoothie now*
> *(shake up your smoothie!)*
> *Twist and Shout (twist and shout!)*
> *C'mon, c'mon, c'mon, drink berry now*
> *(come on, berry!)*
> *Come on and slurp it on out (slurp it on out!)*

But no—if Holly wanted a Twist and Shout, that was what she'd get. Olivia walked over to the line. Brendan was still watching her, and she jerked her head, beckoning him to come and stand next to her. He ran to her like an excited puppy.

Fortunately, Holly had settled in a booth and was scrolling through the photos on her digital camera.

As Ivy's boyfriend caught up with Olivia, she stiffly held out her arms, keeping him at bay.

"Brendan, I—"

His face was lit up like a fireworks display. "When did you get back? Why didn't you tell me? Are you back for good, or just a few days? Why didn't you want me to come over back there?" He ignored her outstretched arms and swept her into a crushing hug that wouldn't have bothered the real Ivy, with her V-strength, but for Olivia, it was totally cutting off her circulation. "This is so exciting!" he breathed into her hair. *Oh no!* "I've missed you so much, you have no idea."

He let go of her at last. Olivia chanced a look back at Holly, who had put her camera down and was watching now. *Ugh. Just what I need.*

Olivia tried not to flinch when Brendan took her hand.

"I'm not Ivy!" she hissed.

Brendan's smile faded. "What are you talking about?"

How could Olivia get him to understand? "It's

me—Olivia! You know, the one who helped you get into the Pall Bearers concert? I answered the question about the third line in the second song on the first album, remember?" That was one detail Ivy couldn't possibly know.

Brendan peered more closely at her. "I don't believe it. For a minute there, I really . . ."

"I have to keep the act up," Olivia said, interrupting him. "Holly can't find out. I've been pretending to be Ivy to help her out. She wants to be a journalist and I didn't want to crush her dreams. She's entering a competition that ends this week. She doesn't know Ivy's in Transylvania. Can you play along with me?"

He sighed and shrugged. "I guess one more game of make-believe won't be such a big deal."

"Thank you!" Olivia gasped. Holly was smiling and waving at them. Olivia waved back.

Brendan grabbed straws while Olivia ordered a Beauty Boosting Blueberry smoothie, a Cherry-O for Brendan, and a Twist and Shout for Holly.

"Coming right up!" said the beaming waitress. No sooner had the order been placed than the entire Mister Smoothie staff—waiters, cashiers, and all—boogied out from behind the counter, snapping their fingers.

> *Well, shake up your smoothie now (shake up*
> *your smoothie!)*
> *Twist and Shout (twist and shout!) ...*

As the whole smoothie shop broke into song, Olivia blushed—very un-Ivy of her.

Holly seemed unfazed. Her camera shutter was clacking away as she took pictures of the whole spectacle. Olivia knew the real Ivy would rather be caught dead than be involved in this!

She tried to will her cheeks back to pale as she made her way over to Brendan and Holly.

"Since when do you order Twist and Shouts?" asked Brendan, his eyes twinkling.

"When in Rome?" replied Olivia, handing out the smoothies. Brendan was really taking his role seriously. Olivia made a mental note to suggest that Brendan look into drama club after this. "Have you two met?" Olivia asked. "Brendan, Holly; Holly, Brendan. Brendan's my, um, boyfriend."

"I can see that," said Holly, grinning broadly. "I don't suppose he gives everyone hugs like that."

Brendan draped an arm across Olivia's shoulders. "Oh, Ivy just loves it when I go and get all romantic!" He laughed and kissed Olivia on the temple. *Don't pull away. Don't pull away!* she willed herself. Holly was still taking photos of them.

"Love's young dream," Holly sighed.

Brendan shrugged. "Something like that. Isn't that right, Ivy?"

What would Ivy do? She dug her elbow sharply into Brendan's ribs. "Quit it with all the mushy stuff," she growled. Brendan laughed.

Okay, now Olivia was officially starting to worry. She knew Brendan Daniels pretty well, and never had she pegged him for this dedicated a thespian.

"So, Brendan," said Olivia, "did you know that Holly here is friends with *Olivia*?" She did exaggerated eye rolls in Holly's direction, hoping that he would catch on. "Remember *Olivia*?"

She just hoped she could get through this little situation without alerting Holly to anything odd. After all, Olivia wasn't doing this to be two-faced. Holly had really helped her and been a true friend; Olivia wanted to do something good back. If she could pull off letting Holly think she'd gotten photos of an übercool Goth like Ivy, then this fiasco would all have been worth it.

"So, Holly," said Brendan, hunching forward. "What brings you to Franklin Grove? Have you been here long? How are you liking it so far?"

But before Holly could answer, Brendan was firing more questions. "Is it cold where you're from? How about the weather here? It's nice, right?" *Easy there, Brendan,* thought Olivia. He was always so laid-back; what had gotten into him? He was practically vibrating in his seat, as if he had too much energy to burn.

Holly pursed her lips. "The weather? Well, I guess it's . . ." Olivia stopped listening because she felt Brendan's fingers intertwining with hers. *Just playing along, right?* Olivia did her best not to pull her hand free, a smile stuck rigidly to her face.

Olivia glanced down at her lap. Their hands were under the table, which meant Holly couldn't see them. And if Holly couldn't see them, then the holding hands wasn't intended to help sell Olivia's cover, which meant . . . Olivia's chest tightened. Did Brendan think she was Ivy for *real*? How was that possible? The tan, the wig, it didn't make sense. And she'd just *told* him that she was Olivia in disguise! Could he have forgotten so quickly? Brendan knew his own girlfriend, didn't he?

That was when she realized—Brendan's hand was blazing in her palm. Now she knew something was wrong. Brendan Daniels should not be heating up like a human radiator. It was no good waiting for Sophia's rescue call now—they had to get out of here as quickly as possible.

"Um, Holly," Olivia interrupted as Holly was explaining something about ozone layers, too much sun, and the Franklin Grove community pool. "I'm really sorry, but I just remembered . . ." She thumped herself on the forehead. "Brendan and I totally have to . . . go do something." Olivia tugged Brendan's hand. "Come on, Brendan, we better get to it."

Brendan flashed Olivia a goofy smile that froze her heart. This was worse than she had thought.

"Okay! Well, next time, then?" Holly said as they wriggled out from the booth. She was only halfway through her Twist and Shout, and Olivia had barely had a chance to touch her drink, but she hauled Brendan as quickly as she could out of Mister Smoothie and into the sunshine. He was chuckling as he allowed himself to be dragged along.

"You're always so impetuous, Ivy," he teased.

"I'm Olivia, remember? Olivia!" she said, slowly and carefully. Brendan just looked confused.

Olivia strode up the street, Brendan in tow. *What am I going to do?* Her heartbeat thrashed and she felt like she couldn't get enough oxygen. She was seriously starting to panic. *Look at him!* Brendan's face was bright red, his hand clammy. She remembered how flushed he'd been before, how much energy he seemed to have. And now his memory seemed to be going! This had to be some kind of ailment that she knew nothing about. She'd once had a Bloodbite Nettle rash, but that was as far as her experience with vampire illnesses went.

She pulled to a stop. "Do you think there's any chance you were exposed to a patch of Bloodbite Nettles?" she asked.

Brendan's smile faded. "Why? What's wrong?"

"*You're* wrong!" she said, prodding a finger into his chest. To her surprise, he staggered back, zigzagging across the sidewalk. "Nettles? Bloodbites?" he asked, his voice slurring. "Ouch!" Brendan had staggered back into a wall and was rubbing his shoulder. His hair fell forward, covering his eyes.

"I think maybe you're right," he muttered. "Something's wrong." He rubbed his hand across his forehead.

"I'm going to get you help," Olivia said, taking hold of his arm. He was burning up!

They started to walk toward Charles's house.

My bio-dad will know what to do, she reassured herself. *He has to!*

☙ CHAPTER 9 ❧

It was after the last class of the day, and Ivy was tapping her boot on the cold slate floor of Miss Avisrova's office. Petra hadn't been in any of the day's lessons, and Ivy wondered what had happened to her. Her vampire friend had probably received nothing more than a slap on the wrist. Ivy was the one Avisrova had it in for.

Six gold-framed portraits hung above Avisrova's claw-footed antique desk, each one featuring a picture of a different old lady, each posing stiffly. The pencils in the iron holder had been sharpened into lethal weapons and the rug was a scary-looking bear hide. In the corner was a polished black coffin. Obviously, Miss Avisrova actually *slept* in her office.

Hanging over an old, varnished wood filing cabinet was a black-and-white class photograph showing young vampires lined up in rows, boys on the left and girls on the right. Ivy peered closer. One boy's face looked familiar—those kind, dark eyes and swept-back hair . . . Yes, there was no mistaking him—it was her dad. Ivy scanned the other faces and recognized another person. The girl on the other side with the tightly pinned bun and stern expression—was that . . . Avisrova? *This is too weird.*

Ivy turned her attention to the bunches of Oxynamon clutched tightly in her hands. She'd snatched them up in the forest, hoping that they could become her excuse if she was found there. She'd planned to say she'd been collect-ing samples for extra credit in Herbal Science. *Like anyone would believe that lame excuse.* But she couldn't help feeling that this wasn't all her fault. Why have an obstacle course there if you didn't want someone to try to complete it? Surely it was a challenge as much as a deterrent, wasn't it?

Avisrova had said something about handing the love letter over in the "customary" way—did that mean that other people had run the Gauntlet, before Ivy?

Yeah right. Wallachia Academy was a school built on thousands of years of tradition. And here she was, thinking one snarky American girl was going to turn all that on its head in one year? *Fat chance.*

She couldn't change Wallachia, and she didn't want Wallachia to change her. So how could it really be the right place for her?

The office door was flung open. Avisrova's monster bat flew in, settled on a windowsill, and stared at Ivy. Then Avisrova herself strutted into the room. *I bet she's here to gloat,* thought Ivy, imagining all the ways her teacher could drag out her detention in order to make it as painful as possible.

Avisrova lowered herself into her high-backed chair. But when the teacher rested her elbows on the desk and her chin on her fists, Ivy got the sense that something was different about her. She didn't look disgusted, like she normally did.

Actually, by the way she was twisting her mouth and knitting her brow, Ivy would have said she looked more curious than anything else.

"Tell me," said Avisrova, relaxing back in her seat. "Why do you have this constant urge to flout authority?"

"I—" Ivy started. Avisrova held up one finger, silencing Ivy immediately.

"And why, exactly, do you get so much pleasure from breaking the rules?" Avisrova scratched her chin with one long, unpainted fingernail.

Ivy waited to make sure Avisrova was done with the loaded questions. "It's not that I enjoy breaking the rules; it's just that when the rules are as strict as they are here, they . . . Well, they break very easily."

Avisrova smiled. It was the first expression Ivy had seen on her face other than a scowl. "You are just like your father was at this age." She sighed.

"My father? Really? Did you know him?"

Avisrova nodded. "I was his . . ." Her gaze slid to one side. *"Classmate."*

Ivy's eyes narrowed. Something in her teacher's voice, in the way she had paused, made Ivy think that Avisrova was being evasive when she said the word *classmate*. Why couldn't she just say what she meant?

"If you are going to be a student here, Ivy *Lazar*, we will have to retrain you. Your insolent American ways will have to go. Wallachia has agreed to accept another Lazar into its illustrious student body, but we must undo your father's grave mistake."

Ivy's breathing hitched. "Grave mistake?"

"The Lazars are one of the few great vampire families left, but rather than stay and raise the next generation here in Transylvania, your father chose to bring you up in the United States. That is not where you belong."

Ivy blinked. "But if it weren't for my father going to America, he would never have met my mother." She realized, as she said it, that this single rogue decision her father had made had shaped their lives and her very existence.

Miss Avisrova slapped her hand on the desk with a loud *bang!* "Exactly." No sooner had she made her outburst than the teacher was folding her hands together in her lap and rearranging her expression into something unreadable. But it was too late. Ivy knew now. There was a history between her teacher and her father.

Did she really want to know the truth? It didn't matter. The pieces of the puzzle were already starting to come together—the reason why Avisrova picked on Ivy and kept referring to her "American ways," like Ivy was some sort of barbarian—because as it turned out, there *was* a reason. Ivy suddenly felt disgusted. *Let's get this punishment over with,* she thought. *Then I can get away from this awful woman.*

"Miss Avisrova, aren't I supposed to be in trouble for my adventure in the woods?"

Ivy thought that Avisrova would jump at the opportunity to scold her. Ivy had given her the perfect opening for a world-class lecture. How could she resist? But Avisrova didn't seem to be angry.

"I'm not going to punish you," she said, pulling open the top drawer of her desk.

"You're not?" asked Ivy slowly. This must be a trick. She watched Avisrova carefully, trying to tell if she was lying.

"It's a shame, but no."

She took out a thin golden necklace with a ruby pendant in the middle and handed it to Ivy. The chain was cold against Ivy's skin. Ivy stared at it, half expecting it to bite her. Now she knew this had to be some kind of test, one of those punishments in disguise that some adults liked to call *lessons*.

"Go on—it's not a trick." Avisrova's half smile was smug. "Surprised? It's your reward," she explained. "This ruby"—she pointed to the red center stone—"was cut from a larger gem that was recovered from the house of Count Gregario, one of the oldest vampires in history and a founding father of Wallachia Academy."

"Thanks," said Ivy, closing her fingers around the necklace. "But I'm not sure I understand. Why am I getting a reward for breaking the rules?"

"Only the bravest souls and most resourceful minds can successfully navigate the Wallachia forest and the Gauntlet that has been created within. Those few who do make their way through are awarded this priceless relic—a piece of a treasure of great importance to the history of our kind. The necklace is meant to act as a symbol of your physical and mental prowess. To receive the ruby necklace of Count Gregario is a huge honor. Only two other former students have ever been awarded it—and you have met them both."

Ivy gasped. "Is one of them my dad?"

Avisrova nodded. "Yes, Charles is one of them."

Ivy racked her brain. What other vampires did she know who could have completed the Gauntlet? Avisrova stayed quiet at her desk. Then the answer came to Ivy. "You?" she whispered, not quite sure she could believe what she was saying. "You're the other student?"

A wistful smile passed over her teacher's lips. "Karl and I—well, Charles and I—we found each other in the forest, both trying to get to the other side. Karl was going one way, and I the other. When we stumbled across each other, we swapped tips about terrain. We both made it through, with the other's help. I'm not sure either of us could have finished like you did, alone."

Ivy tried to picture her Etiquette teacher dodging trip wires and swinging through trees. Was this the same woman who had been lecturing her about the correct arm position for ballroom dancing only one day earlier? Ivy felt her whole attitude toward Miss Avisrova shift.

"But—but . . . you've been so furious at me for breaking rules!" Ivy spluttered. "And you did the same thing?"

The Etiquette teacher cocked her head to one side. "Furious? Or impressed? I never said anything you were doing was wrong. I said, 'Bravo!' and gave you a round of applause. Does that sound like disapproval to you?"

"But your tone of voice . . . It was so mean!" Ivy protested. She discovered that in her excited state, she'd gotten to her feet.

Her teacher shrugged. "A lifetime of teaching at the Academy makes it difficult for me to . . . soften my manner. I apologize. I don't want every pupil knowing what challenges lie at the heart of Wallachia. So few are capable of meeting them, I don't want my girls to be disappointed. But you . . . I knew you'd be different—that you'd have spirit."

Ivy could just imagine what Brendan would have to say to that: "Oh yes, Ivy has spirit, all right." She wondered what her boyfriend was doing right now, and felt a wave of homesickness.

"Love isn't invincible," Miss Avisrova continued. It was like she could read Ivy's thoughts. But was she really thinking about Charles Vega? "Love is sometimes fragile."

"I know that much," Ivy said. "My sister, Olivia, was crazy about her boyfriend. She had the perfect Hollywood romance. Seriously, it was like *Cinderella*. But the distance between them . . ." Ivy's voice trailed off. She knew that if she kept talking, she would start to wonder what the future held for her and Brendan. Ivy was crazy about her boyfriend, but they had an ocean between them and no private plane like Jackson to take them back and forth! "So, anyway, um . . . well, thanks," she finished, snatching up her Oxynamon and dropping the ruby necklace into the pocket of her skirt.

Her hand was on the doorknob when she heard Avisrova say, "We first locked eyes on the polo field." The teacher had pulled an ancient photo album from her desk drawer and was flicking through the pages.

Ivy exhaled, returning to her seat. Yuck, she did not want to hear about her dad's former love life! Olivia would be so much more into this gooey-gooey love story stuff. But how could Ivy leave Avisrova all alone with her memories? *I'll just stay a little bit,* she thought, stroking the red jewel she'd been given with one finger. She couldn't help feeling proud of her achievements in the forest—and Avisrova had given her the credit she'd deserved. The least she could do was listen to her teacher's story.

* 🦇 *

An hour later, Ivy sat in her open coffin with her laptop on her knees. Her stomach was growling. Avisrova's reminiscences had gone on forever, and when she'd finally finished telling Ivy about the time she and Charles had won the Academy three-legged race together, Ivy had sprinted vampire-fast to the Wallachia Canteen, only to find that the staff had already stopped serving and had the chairs propped upside down on top of the tables.

Luckily, I didn't miss much, anyway. Meat loaf with blood-infused ketchup and plasma-filled dinner rolls wasn't exactly one of her favorite meals.

Ivy rubbed her feet on the soft red velour lining of her coffin. Why wasn't anyone signed on to Lonely Echo? She refreshed her list of friends in the sidebar, but no familiar names popped up with the little green "available" sign. Ivy trawled the Vorld Vide Veb, checking up on some of her favorite blogs—Vintage Vampire and Transylvania Teen.

After she'd learned all she could about celebrity director Harker's latest film release, *Setting Sun*, along with the entire cast's makeup secrets, Ivy returned to Lonely Echo. It was weird for *all* her friends to be missing, and to make matters worse, her in-box was like a ghost town. Something big had to be happening in Franklin Grove—something big that Ivy knew nothing about. That could be the only explanation—*But what could it be?*

Her chest throbbed. She'd been fighting this feeling off as long as she could, but she had to come clean with herself. The truth was, Ivy felt disconnected being so far from home. Without

Olivia, it was like half of her was missing, and without Brendan, she felt like part of her heart was on the other side of the globe.

It wasn't simple homesickness or that she thought the school was snooty—*although it totally is.* This place just wasn't her. Ivy Vega didn't wear cable-knit cardigans, she wasn't afraid to talk to boys, and she didn't eat hamburgers with a knife and fork.

She had thought it would be cool to connect with her vampy roots, but the school's rules were so strict she hadn't had any time to spend with her grandparents at all. *And what roots are more important than those in my own family tree?*

What was the point? Ivy leaned her head back in the coffin. She hadn't even made any real friends.

Footsteps charged into her room. Ivan started flapping wildly, and Ivy nearly leaped out of her coffin.

"Ivy? Ivy?" Petra was breathless.

"Over here." Ivy waved.

Petra had a rucksack slung over her shoulder.

She took it off, grabbed the bottom of it, and shook it out violently. Tupperware containers of all shapes and sizes spilled out onto their floor. Petra kneeled on the ground and started to sort them. "I didn't know what you liked!" Petra seemed flustered by the array of sandwiches, cakes, entrées, and pastries. "So I grabbed everything I could."

Ivy laughed. "Aren't you going to get in trouble?"

"Are you kidding me?" Petra handed Ivy a slice of chocolate cake and a fork. "After what you did for me, I owe you everything. You, Ivy Vega, are the bravest, most selfless girl I know. You made it through the Gauntlet! I bow to you!" Petra made a grand gesture of performing exaggerated bows as if worshipping Ivy.

Ivy felt her face get hot. "Okay, enough, enough!" She giggled. "I get it. You're totally welcome."

Petra sat back on her heels. "Etan sent me a love letter! A beautiful love letter! Here, let me read it for you." Petra coughed twice, unfolding a wrinkled letter. "Ahem," she began to read.

Dear my loveliest flower, Petra,

My heart yearns for the time when we can be close. You are the sharp point to my fang. The wind beneath my bat wings. The tombstone in my crypt.

Forever and always yours,
Etan

Petra hugged the paper, swaying back and forth. "Can you believe that? Is that not just the most romantic thing you've ever heard?"

Gag me, thought Ivy, thankful that her mouth was full with a big bite of cake so that she couldn't speak. The letter was *way* too over-the-top for Ivy's taste. But in matters of the heart, to each her own.

"I know. I was speechless, too," said Petra, placing her hand on Ivy's shoulder. "But he likes me! It's official—he really likes me back! And none of this would have happened if you hadn't finished the Gauntlet."

Ivy hugged her. "Thanks for thinking of me

with all this food. I thought I was going to die of hunger!"

"No problem." Petra beamed. "Now, excuse me . . ." She wiggled her eyebrows. "But I just have to go and frame this!"

She hurried out of the room, flourishing her love letter above her head. Ivy watched her leave. Petra was turning out to be a much better friend than Ivy had first imagined. It seemed like she didn't just want to use Ivy as a cover—she really was grateful to her. *Maybe this place isn't so bad, after all.*

Ivy climbed back into her coffin. She was just about to shut her laptop down when she heard the ping of Lonely Echo. *Finally!*

She clicked the screen and saw a pale, washed-out Olivia. "Ivy," she said. "I'm so glad I caught up with you." Something in the tone of her voice tied Ivy's stomach in knots. "I've got some news."

CHAPTER 10

Olivia was going to need a week's worth of Beautilicious under-eye treatment cream to get these bags to go away. Bending closer to the mirror, she prodded the two dark circles. Then she pulled away and looked around the room. Nobody else looked any better.

Olivia was curled up in an armchair at her bio-dad's house. Brendan was asleep and drooling on the silk couch, while his parents snored on a cramped love seat nearby.

They'd been up all night. Olivia's first instinct had been to take Brendan to the hospital right away, but she'd suddenly remembered that no way could she bring her sister's boyfriend to a bunny hospital. That might expose the vampire secret.

Instead, Olivia had succeeded in getting Brendan to the Vegas' house, after which Charles had inspected him and confirmed her worst fears—Brendan was seriously ill. Charles had insisted Brendan stay there, since the Vegas' home was bigger and everyone would be more comfortable. Plus, he had a well-stocked vampire medicine cabinet—not that it seemed to be doing any good. Brendan had been passed out for hours. The only sign of life was a slight twitch in his fingers. Of course, his complexion always looked corpse-like to Olivia. That much hadn't changed. But seeing him lie there so helpless? Olivia thought even Ivy would be scared. She'd told her sister as much as she had dared over the Internet—how Brendan was sick but they were all taking care of him. She hadn't told Ivy exactly *how* sick, though. *What can she do in Transylvania anyway?*

Olivia smelled bacon frying and waffles cooking. Charles was in the kitchen making breakfast, but Olivia doubted that anyone had much of an appetite. She clutched her stomach and rocked in the chair. She was worried sick about Brendan—literally!

The worst part was that she'd noticed that things had seemed off for days with Brendan—the gray patches of skin, the feverishness, the fast talking—but she hadn't managed to put two and two together until yesterday. Now she felt awful for not asking questions earlier. Olivia watched the sleeping Brendan. Even though she knew it was silly, she crossed her fingers, squeezed her eyes shut, and made a wish. *Please let him be okay!*

She tried to cheer herself up—nobody else had guessed what was wrong with him, so how could she, a mere bunny, have realized that he had a vampire illness? She may be related to vampires by blood, but vamp biology was way beyond her area of expertise.

The doorbell rang, the classical organ music sounding somber from the big hallway.

"Olivia, can you get that?" Charles popped out of the kitchen holding a greasy spatula.

"Coming!" Olivia ran to the door and opened

it to see Holly standing there with her hands on her hips.

"Hello, Olivia," Holly greeted her stiffly.

"Um, hi," Olivia said. Something was obviously wrong—but what? She'd climbed out of Ivy's clothes and the stupid wig. But still, Holly seemed strained. Everything had been fine when "Ivy" had left her. Was she mad that Olivia had been a no-show? "Um . . . how did you find this house?" she asked. She knew she'd never shared Ivy's address with Holly, so her new friend must have been doing some serious detective work.

"Oh, you know, I asked around." Holly flipped her red-streaked hair over one shoulder. "I'm good at that sort of thing."

"Okay . . . well, it's great to see you, but this really isn't a—"

"I just wanted to return Ivy's phone to her," said Holly. She wiggled Olivia's rhinestone-covered phone in front of her face. Olivia felt her eyes widen. She'd been in such a hurry to get Brendan out of Mister Smoothie that she'd forgotten to grab her phone from the table, which meant . . . "I had a most interesting conversation with somebody named Sophia?" One of Holly's eyebrows was raised. "Funny thing—she seemed to think she'd called *you* and not Ivy."

Olivia's mouth went dry.

Holly gave Olivia a tight-lipped smile. "I guess that you and Ivy must be so identical even your phone numbers look alike, huh?"

"That's right," said a familiar voice from behind Holly. "Only one digit is different. Our friends mess it up all the time." Olivia looked past Holly to see Ivy walking up the stone steps to her father's mansion, rolling her darkly lined eyes. "Super annoying."

Olivia's jaw dropped. *What?* She tried to resist the urge to run up and tackle her sister. "Hey, Ivy," she said instead, trying to play it cool. "I didn't expect you to be here so . . . soon." *That was an understatement!* Olivia hadn't known that Ivy was planning to come home at all!

Ivy was carrying a heavy rucksack slung over her back and a straw bag with an exotic-looking plant spilling out the top in long tendrils. A dazzling ruby-and-gold necklace sparkled at her throat. Olivia made a mental note to ask Ivy where she'd gotten it once things had calmed down.

Ivy smiled at Holly. "It's great to see you again." *Thank goodness for vampire hearing,* thought Olivia, realizing that Ivy must have picked up on the conversation while walking up the pathway. "I'd love to stay and talk some more, but my dad needs me inside."

As Ivy disappeared inside the house, she winked at Olivia. The last thing Olivia heard was her sister calling out, "Dad, do we have any lavender?"

"Oh my gosh, I'm so sorry!" Holly's mouth was open and she looked horrified. "I had never seen you together and I thought that maybe you were some weirdo who pretended she had a twin, or worse, like, a practical joker. I didn't mean to . . . I mean, I just thought that . . . I thought you were making fun of me!" Holly buried her face in her hands, and when she emerged again, her eyes were glistening. "The only reason I made a big deal about the phone thing was that I thought you were being mean." She lifted her chin and wiped smudged mascara from underneath her eyes. "I stand up for myself and, well . . . I was so sure I was right."

"It's okay, Holly." Olivia patted her back. "I completely understand. I know someone just like that, so it's not a big deal. I promise." If only Olivia could tell Holly the truth! She had only been trying to help when she'd pulled her switcheroo. But a long time ago, Ivy had broken the most important vamp rule, the First Law of the Night—*Thou shall not reveal one's true self to an outsider*—so that the twins could be closer, and Olivia was not going to be the one to risk the secrecy of all vampire society. Besides, she and Holly were getting along fine now. *Why rock the boat? Maybe after this we can have a clean slate together.*

She smiled at Holly. "Hey, I hate to run, but we're kind of in the middle of a . . . family thing." Olivia chewed her lip, inwardly cringing at another kind-of-sort-of lie. *This is the last one, I swear!* She was glad to have a new friend, but if there was one thing she'd learned over the past few days, it was how important Ivy was to her.

"Sure—of course!" said Holly. She smiled and turned back up the path. "See you around. And sorry, again."

Olivia closed the door, thankful that she'd somehow managed to skate by with her new friendship intact.

Inside, Olivia found Ivy kneeling by Brendan's side with her hand on his forehead. Olivia hadn't seen her sister look so anxious since she had gotten sick in Transylvania.

"Ivy?" Olivia asked gently, rubbing her twin's back.

Ivy took Olivia's hand and got to her feet. They hugged and Olivia wished that she never had to let her sister go. But Ivy broke the moment. "I have something I need to do for Brendan in the kitchen," she said, casting one last glance in her boyfriend's direction before pulling a leafy plant from her pocket. "Can you grab me a bowl?"

Thankful to finally be doing something useful, Olivia followed her into the kitchen, hurried over to a cabinet, and pulled out a large silver mixing bowl.

Ivy sprinkled the weird plant into the bowl, then began mashing it and stirring in lavender. Charles and Olivia watched her work.

"What is that plant?" asked Olivia, giving the mixture a sniff.

"That's Oxynamon." Ivy pushed the pestle harder into the leaves.

Olivia pinched a bit between her fingers. "Oxy-what?"

Ivy gently slapped her hand and Olivia dropped the plant back into the bowl. "Before I left, I ran Brendan's symptoms by Helga. She's working as the Herbal Science teacher at Wallachia now. This is what she recommended."

"For what?" Olivia watched as Ivy sprinkled some more of the lavender into the Oxynamon bowl.

"Apparently, Brendan's symptoms are classic signs of a platelet disorder. He probably got it by eating something with too many artificial preservatives. It can be very serious for a vampire." Ivy shook the bowl, mixing the ingredients.

"Of course!" Olivia smacked her head. "A few days ago Brendan said he had a stomachache after he'd eaten that Taurus Bar." Olivia shuddered at the memory of the bar's foul smell. How could anyone expect to put that in their mouth and *not* get sick?

Ivy nodded. "That sounds like the culprit. Energy products are processed and chock-full of artificial ingredients. Brendan's system probably couldn't handle them all. He should have known better."

Olivia whistled. "Who are you and what did you do with my sister?" she teased. "You're a genius!"

Charles left the room for a moment and came back holding a Taurus Bar. "Is this what Brendan ate, Olivia?" he asked.

"Yes! Where'd you get that?"

"I checked Brendan's jacket pockets and saw that he had a spare one. Who knows how many of these he's been eating." Charles read the label. "It contains oxymistine."

"What's that?" asked Olivia. Brendan had made it sound as if the bar would be good for both humans and vampires.

"It's a chemical that gives vampires energy,

the same way humans get a boost from caffeine. It should be harmless enough, but judging by Brendan's state, there must be a lot more in these bars than the 1.4 grams advertised on the label." He unwrapped the bar and broke a piece off, studying it in the overhead light. "Hmm . . . very suspicious."

"Don't worry about that right now, Detective Dad." Ivy winked. "The remedy will be ready any second." She took another pinch of lavender and added it to the mix, wafting some of the fragrance up to her nose and sniffing.

Olivia smiled. "I remember how you cured me when I was in . . . Wait a minute! We still haven't talked about why you're back here in Franklin Grove. You're supposed to be"— she pointed outside—"and now you're"—Olivia pointed down at her feet. "But how did . . ." She shook her head and stamped her ballet flats. "What's going on?!"

"I promise I'll explain everything." Ivy scooped the bowl under her arm. "Right after I fix up my boyfriend."

"Did you know she was coming?" Olivia

demanded, looking at Charles.

His eyes crinkled at the corners. "I had to buy her a plane ticket, didn't I? Ivy called me last night and said she wanted to come home. So here she is."

Olivia stared dumbfounded at the swinging kitchen door. But it didn't matter. *I don't care why she's back, so long as she's back. My life gets crazy when she's not around!*

★ 🦇 ★

Ivy sat on the edge of the sofa, holding Brendan's hand. She couldn't believe how feverish he'd been before, but his skin was much cooler now. Ivy took in his marble face and the dark shaggy hair that brushed his cheek as he slept. The dimple on his chin was just as cute as she'd remembered it, though she wouldn't admit that to anyone in a million years. Ivy was so glad to see him she could hardly understand how she'd managed to say good-bye in the first place.

It would be a few hours before he woke up, which was fine because she still had a lot to wrap her jet-lagged brain around. Fortunately, his parents had crashed in a bedroom, so she didn't have to worry about making polite conversation with anyone. "So you're sure you're okay?" she asked Olivia, who was sitting cross-legged on the Oriental rug with their dad.

Charles had brought in a tray full of mugs of rich hot chocolate. He blew on the tops of them to cool them down.

"Yes!" Olivia repeated. "I told you, the breakup really was mutual. Jackson . . ." Olivia paused when she mentioned his name. "Jackson is a good guy. We'll still be friends. And I know one thing: We made his thousands of adoring fans happy!"

Leave it to Olivia to find the positive spin. "But I wasn't here to—" Ivy protested.

"I survived," Olivia reassured her. "And besides, what we should be focused on is Dad's big day! Remember the whole wedding thing?"

"It's not just my big day." Charles patted Olivia on the head. "It will be a big day for all of us. We're getting a new Vega." He jiggled open the thin drawer in the coffee table and pulled out a magazine called *Vampire Bride*, flipping it open to a page on which a slender female vampire was riding a camel next to the pyramids in a formfitting wedding dress. "Now, what do you think of this, Ivy?"

"I think, 'Hooray, more wedding planning,'" Ivy joked. "My favorite."

Olivia tossed a throw pillow at her.

"Hey, watch it! I'm only kidding!" It was true. Ivy was totally thrilled her dad was getting married to Lillian. She had often worried that her father would never find a match. But somehow, it seemed that ever since she'd found Olivia, her family managed to keep getting bigger and better.

Ivy's cheeks weren't used to all this smiling, but she couldn't stop, even when her face started to hurt. How did she ever think she could live anywhere but Franklin Grove? She looked from her dad to Olivia to Brendan. *This is where I belong.*

Charles handed her a cup of cocoa. "You know, there might be some serious questions asked by people at the Academy about your departure." He took a swig from his own mug. "And I'm fairly certain your grandparents are going to be upset. It was their dream that you attend Wallachia."

"I know," said Ivy, pulling her knees to her chest. "But it wasn't *my* dream."

Charles nodded thoughtfully. "And I'm extremely proud of you for giving the school a fair shot and for making up your own mind about it."

"I met one of your old classmates, Dad." Ivy watched Charles carefully to gauge his reaction. "Alexandra Avisrova?" Even now Ivy could barely say the name without shuddering.

"Ah," said Charles. His face was smooth, serene yet thoughtful. "Yes, Alexandra . . . she was a . . . a good friend of mine from school, yes. We no longer keep in touch."

Ivy wanted to press him for more details, but she sensed that her father wasn't going to provide any, so she changed the subject. "And my grandparents? Will they be disappointed in me?" That had been her biggest fear about her decision to leave Wallachia.

"Your grandparents will understand," said Charles. "They only want what is best for you."

"Absolutely," said Olivia, scooping up a spoonful of marshmallows and plopping them in her cup. "And anyway, it looks like the Academy has already served its purpose."

"What do you mean?" Ivy asked.

"I mean, look how well you've taken to vampire medicine! I can see it now: Ivy Vega, Vampire Doc. Oh!" Olivia clapped. "That would make an awesome TV medical drama."

Charles and Ivy laughed. "Okay, but I'll probably stick with Ivy Vega, Franklin Grove Student, for now."

"That's a relief," said Olivia, and grinned.

Charles raised his mug. "To family," he said. Ivy leaned in and they all clinked cups. At this, Brendan's eyelashes fluttered. "Ivy?" he mumbled. "Is Ivy in Transylvania?" Brendan blinked against the light.

Ivy leaned down and kissed his clammy forehead. "No, she's home," she said. "And she promises never, ever to go away again."

Sienna Mercer lives in Toronto, Canada, with her two cats, Calypso and Angel. She does most of her writing in her attic, surrounded by photos she's taken on her travels. She doesn't have a twin sister, but always wished that she did.

POISON APPLE BOOKS

The Dead End

This Totally Bites!

Miss Fortune

Now You See Me...

Midnight Howl

Her Evil Twin

Curiosity Killed the Cat

At First Bite

THRILLING.

BONE-CHILLING.

THESE BOOKS

HAVE BITE!

HERE'S A
SPINE-TINGLING SNEAK PEEK!

Over a delicious dinner of perfectly cooked hamburgers, Great-aunt Margo talked about her hometown in Romania. A small village with a funny name, it was nestled deep in the Carpathian Mountains, and it sounded beautiful. Margo described lush green forests, clear blue streams, narrow cobblestone streets, and ancient castles.

As she spoke — and Mom chimed in with memories of photographs her parents had shown her — I glanced out the window at the Manhattan skyline. Though I loved the tall buildings and concrete sidewalks of New York City, I liked the idea of such a rural, quaint place . . . the place my ancestors had lived! Suddenly, I realized that Great-aunt Margo had given me a great starting point for my social studies project.

Excited, I helped with the dishes and excused myself for the night. Then I headed into my room, grabbed my laptop, and sat cross-legged on my bed.

I opened Google, then typed in the name of my family's Romanian village, grateful for the *Did you mean?* feature after I'd misspelled it twice. Then I clicked on the Wikipedia page; it showed a pretty picture of the forests Great-aunt Margo had talked about, and gave the basic facts: population, map coordinates, and weather. Then, as I skimmed the page, I spotted a sentence that made my jaw drop.

> *Located in the region once known as Transylvania, this small town is still home to many vampire legends.*

I sat back, my pulse racing. *Transylvania*? As in, Count Dracula territory? I had no idea that my family came from *there*."